WITHDRAWN

Henri Lopes, the eminent Congolese writer, was born in 1937 in Kinshasa. He received his secondary and university education in France, but returned to the Congo Republic to teach history in a school in Brazzaville.

His teaching career was curtailed when he was appointed to the Congo-Brazzaville Government. Through a succession of senior ministerial positions – Minister of Education, Foreign Affairs, Finance and between 1973–4 Prime Minister – he was afforded an insider's view of African politics. His experiences in government are reflected in his enlightened and often satirical portrayals of characters in this collection of short stories.

In addition to *Tribaliques*, which won the Grand Prix Littéraire de l'Afrique Noire in 1972, and is translated here for the first time, Henri Lopes' writings include poetry and three novels.

Henri Lopes is currently living in Paris and working as Assistant Director General for Culture and Communication at UNESCO.

HENRI LOPES

TRIBALIKS

CONTEMPORARY CONGOLESE STORIES

Translated by Andrea Leskes

HEINEMANN

Heinemann Educational Books Ltd.
22 Bedford Square, London WC1B HH

Heinemann Educational Books Inc.
70 Court Street, Portsmouth, New Hampshire, 03801, USA
Heinemann Educational Books (Nigeria) Ltd.
PMB 5205, Ibadan
Heinemann Educational Books (Kenya) Ltd.
Kijabe Street, PO Box 45314, Nairobi
Heinemann Educational Boleswa
PO Box 10103, Village Post Office, Gaborone, Botswana
heinemann Educational Books (Caribbean) Ltd.
175 Mountain View Avenue, Kingston 6, Jamaica

EDINBURGH MELBOURNE AUCKLAND
SINGAPORE KUALA LUMPUR NEW DELHI

British Library Cataloguing in Publication Data
Lopes, Henri
Tribaliks.—(African writers series).
I. Title II. Tribaliques. *English*
III. Series
843[F]   PQ3989.2.L65

ISBN 0–435–90762–X
ISBN 0–435–90763–8 Pbk

Printed in Great Britain by
Richard Clay Ltd, Bungay, Suffolk

CONTENTS

PREFACE

This work was undertaken in the belief that Henri Lopes' writing is timely and of interest to an English language public. Throughout the translation, I was strongly supported by Thomas Cassirer, Micheline Dufau and Richard Tedeschi, all faculty members in the Department of French and Italian at the University of Massachusetts, Amherst. Their help and criticism were invaluable. Vivian Leskes Ward acted as my first line of defence against Gallicisms. A grant from the Ludwig Vogelstein Foundation aided in the final stages of manuscript preparation.

A.L.
Hanover, New Hampshire

INTRODUCTION

Henri Lopes is an important contemporary literary and political figure from the People's Republic of the Congo. He belongs to the younger generation of African authors of French expression; those authors who began writing after their countries achieved independence in the 1960s. Since all his books have so far been released by African publishers, and until recently none have been available in translation, he is little known outside Africa. Yet within Africa, Lopes' work has received notable acclaim. *Tribaliques*, the collection of short stories from which this translation was derived, saw and continues to see enormous popular and critical success. Originally published in 1971 and in its eighth printing in 1983, the book received the prestigious *Grand prix littéraire de l'Afrique noire* in 1972.

Born in neighbouring Kinshasa (then the Belgian Congo) in 1937, Lopes was brought up in the urban environments of Brazzaville and Bangui. He completed secondary school and attended university in France where he was a leader of the extreme leftist Federation of Black African Students in France (FEANF). With both university and post-graduate degrees in hand, he returned to the Congo in 1964. He taught history, and then served as head of the history department at the *École Normale Supérieure d'Afrique Noire* in Brazzaville. Like many other European-educated Africans, Lopes entered politics and rapidly acceded to important ministerial positions. He served as Minister of Education, Prime Minister and Finance Minister under several presidents before more or less retiring from active Congolese political life in 1979. He is currently based in Paris as UNESCO's Assistant Director General for Culture and Communication.

Since the political and social situation of his country serves Lopes as a source of inspiration for many elements of his stories, a basic familiarity with the recent history of the Congo will help provide the context for his work and explain many references.

Contemporary Congolese History

The People's Republic of the Congo was part of French Equatorial Africa from 1885 to 1960, when the French colonial empire in Africa was dismantled. In that year the Congo-Brazzaville, as it is also called, was granted independence, but chose to remain within the French community.

The first President of the newly independent Congo, Abbé Fulbert Youlou, advocated close ties with the former colonial power. Popular dissatisfaction with his administration forced Youlou out of power in August 1963 through an event still referred to as the Congo's revolution, 'The Three Glorious Days'. His opponents, a coalition of military officers, union leaders and students, accused Youlou of an extravagant life style, reactionary policies and widespread government corruption[1]. Lopes draws on political history such as this to help mould the fictitious president, Takana, in the story 'The Veteran'. Takana's negative traits recall those attributed to Youlou.

The new leaders, many of whom had their political views shaped in France during their sojourn there as students, repudiated what was seen as Youlou's neo-colonialism. They established a one-party state and in 1964 proclaimed scientific socialism as their national ideology[2]. Since then, the Congo has been a Marxist state. Ties with France have, however, remained strong as French commercial enterprises played an important role in the independent Congo, and France continued to supply technical advisers. The French presence in post-independence Congo is evident in two of the stories in this collection, 'Whiskey' and 'The Honourable Gentleman'.

The 1970s witnessed a presidential assassination followed by a military dictatorship and intra-party fighting. In 1979, popular election brought Denis Sassou N'Guesso to the presidency, a position he still holds.

Instability in the economic and social affairs of the new Congo state paralleled that of its politics. When they crossed the threshold of independence in 1960, the African people found themselves thrown into power and forced to assume the active role in creating a cohesive, viable society. This new society, built on top of both the traditional, pre-colonial patterns and the residual influences from the century of colonization, faced constant cultural bombardment from the modern, urban Western world. These multiple and contradictory pressures caused a state of disequilibrium as the African societies tried to define their national identities.

Yet the coming of independence did not free the majority of Africans from domination. Oppression of two types now existed side by side. Since European economic, technical, cultural and educational influence remained strong, the African countries were still highly dependent and racially motivated oppression continued. In addition, often the new black political leaders were more concerned with personal gain than with the welfare of their countries. They joined in partnership with the financial interests of the former colonial powers which continued to exploit natural resources and manpower. Tribal differences and conflicts led to the institutionalization of tribally motivated oppression. Development was hindered by ethnic and regional divisions[3]. In the worst cases of this neo-colonialism, unenlightened black leaders were no less oppressive than the former white rulers they replaced; only the colour of their skin was different. Lopes' reference in 'The Veteran' to an inner circle of presidential advisers catering to the interests of a particular ethnic group is based on historical occurrences.

During this period of rapid evolution, one of the major

social forces operating throughout Africa was the demographic movement into the cities. The urbanization of Africa, brought about through contact with European culture, pulled the racial and ethnic conflicts of pre-colonial Africa into the modern world and transformed them into an important social force. Cities, historically the world's melting pots, provided the environment where people from different tribes were thrown together in new and unique ways. Yet the traditional, ingrained prejudices remained. It was in the cities, the milieu in which Lopes himself was raised and about which he writes, that the tribal conflicts were magnified.

Lopes the Writer

In his writing, Henri Lopes focuses on the problems confronting contemporary Africa. He believes that in order for Africans to solidify their independence and move ahead towards the creation of an egalitarian, modern state, they must recognize their weaknesses, root them out and restructure society.

His message is didactic and to reinforce its educational value, Lopes writes simply, in a style easily comprehensible to a large public. His message is also socially relevant; his eye is focused outward to society, rather than inward for self-analysis.

Lopes assigns himself the role of analyst, pointing his finger at the problems he considers common to most African countries. He speaks to all Africans and attempts to awaken their consciousness. Lopes can be called a social realist. He observes society around him, draws on real life to create fictional situations, and then mirrors reality by illustrating the effect of society's problems on individual private lives. His characters are often from his own class: the educated, urban elite, the so-called *evolués* who are the most westernized segment of African society. They are the country's administrators and professionals, who speak French and in many ways live like Europeans. Yet despite their privileged position, they are still subjected to the effects of the neo-colonialist structure and often chafe at being governed by corrupt leaders, highly placed but mediocre at best. Kalala, the protagonist in 'Whiskey', is representative of this class.

Of the numerous problems faced by contemporary African society, Henri Lopes concentrates on three which he considers important factors inhibitory to the development of an egalitarian, modern state:
– tribalism and political power
– the situation of modern African women
– the attitude towards education.

All three of these themes are introduced in *Tribaliks*, his first book, and each becomes the major focus of one of his subsequent works.

In selecting the word *Tribaliques* as the French title for his short stories, Lopes focuses our attention on 'tribalism', underlining its importance as a major destabilizing, divisive factor in the social and political climate of contemporary African society. 'Tribalism' refers to the 'defense of a so-called "tribal" interest in contrast to a larger interest'[4]. The negative aspects of tribal society are what divide one tribe from another and lead to tribalism: prejudices, tribal rivalries, favouritism, provincialism. The 'tribe' can be contrasted to the 'nation': tribalism to nationalism. Adoption by African countries of the nation as the important political and social entity (a Western concept), can be seen as an important step towards Westernization and modernization. Lopes feels that tribalism interferes with this nation building.

The notion of tribalism is central to *Tribaliks*, although in most stories of the collection it plays only a minor, albeit recurring, role. Glimpsed in passing are traditional prejudices, nepotism and preferential treatment of tribal brothers, all of which were encouraged by the colonial rulers in their attempt to play one tribe against another (the divide and conquer philosophy).

Lopes' clear, honest, satirically critical comments on the political structure of post-independence Africa are among the strongest elements of his work. They appear in most of his short stories, play at least subsidiary roles in all his novels, and become the *raison d'être* of his most recent book, *Le Pleurer-Rire* (*The Laughing Cry*, Readers International, 1987). Lopes denounces corrupt officials, political opportunism, unqualified civil servants, torture, collusion with foreign financial interests, mediocrity, and political cronyism.

The cultural tensions and upheavals of contemporary African society are nowhere more evident than in the situation of Africa's women. Although the traditional, feminine role varies somewhat across the African continent,[5] African women have always been considered as valuable to society. Yet their worth has been mostly as a productive force (workhorses) and as a reproductive force (childbearers)[6,7]. Although scholars disagree as to the extent of respect and liberty accorded women in traditional pre-colonial society, it can hardly be denied that colonization did little to improve the status of women. Rather, to the contrary, the gap between male and female freedoms widened since men had greater access to education[8] and economic opportunities[9] and women, in addition to the prejudices and inequalities of the past, came face to face with those associated with present-day underdevelopment[10]. African women have largely been deprived of formal education, constrained by tradition and under the authority of first their fathers and then their husbands. Polygamy is widespread. Marriages are arranged alliances between clans in which the women have little or no say.

In four of the stories in *Tribaliks*, African women play major roles, and their situation becomes the focal point for Lopes' second book, *La Nouvelle Romance*. Many of Lopes' female characters are sympathetically drawn modern African women: young, educated in European-style schools, and intellectually alert. His attitude toward them is neither paternalistic nor chauvinistic. Women are portrayed as positive forces, necessary to the creation of a modern Africa, rather than as poetic objects representing either the humiliated continent or the hope of the race. For Lopes, the oppression of the African woman is part of the oppression of all women, and this in its turn is indissociable from the oppression of humankind. He believes that Africa cannot expect to move into the modern world and at the same time keep her women undereducated and oppressed. The independence of Africa and the freedom of her women are inexorably intertwined. Lopes seems convinced that true African liberation will not happen until her women enjoy freedom and equality.

Lopes' interest in the role of education and the educator in developing nations is both personal and profound. Improved education should be a national priority and, in his stories, Lopes deplores the lack of student commitment and the low level of respect accorded to teachers. His third book, *Sans Tam-Tam*, is an elegy in praise of the educator; the role of education takes on major importance.

Henri Lopes' literary techniques and inspiration have their roots in both African and Western traditions. Yet it cannot be denied that despite Western literary influences, his work has a strong African flavour. The situations described reflect the modern African experience. His viewpoint is that of an insider, one who has lived and suffered through the realities about which he writes. Although critical of the social situation, Lopes is nonetheless understanding of the plight of the individuals caught in its snares. He does not condemn. Rather he uses his skill to draw for his readers detailed, realistic pictures of individual lives.

Lopes states that he writes in French, albeit only a minority in the Congo speak and read the language, simply because it is the language in which he feels most comfortable[11]. Further, he feels that each writer should let artistic integrity dictate his language of expressions[12]. Yet clearly Lopes is addressing an African audience; specifically those Africans sufficiently educated to read literature, and therefore to read a European language. Africans obviously see themselves reflected in his books since he has experienced such great popularity across French-speaking Africa. Familiarity with Lopes' social philosophy leads us to conclude, however, that French additionally represents for him the language of a unified, modern Congolese nation; it is through the possession of European languages that Africans wield power[12].

In several interviews, Lopes has expressed definite views on the role of the writer in contemporary Africa[11,13,14] He sees literature as a means to awaken political consciousness and the writer as an activist in that he induces others to act. The writer should express his reactions to society around him and contribute to the building of a modern nation[13]. Yet Lopes thinks as a Pan-Africanist rather than as a nationalist, and in an even larger sense, as a universalist. The Third World crosses frontiers and political barriers and all its people should work together towards true liberation.

Translator's Notes

Like most other African authors who write in French, Henri Lopes' characters generally speak standard French (his latest book, *Le Pleurer-Rire* is an exception). He distinguishes between personalities and social classes by differences in tone and level of language. In *Tribaliques*, Lopes does not pidginize French. The translation was designed to follow Lopes' usage closely and expresses Africa through situation rather than through African syntax or lexical elements. The few African words Lopes himself used were retained in the translation.

All translation is interpretation. 'Each act of translation is one of approximation'[14]. If we attempt a translation with the hope of accomplishing perfect transference from one language/culture to another, we are bound to meet with frustration. This is especially true in the translation of a work about a culture written in a language which is in some respects foreign to the reality of that culture. The current book is a case in point. Lopes speaks about Africa but uses the French language as his instrument to do so. Although French is an integral part of the twentieth-century Congo, it is associated with, and reflective of, certain aspects of Congolese reality more than others. The author himself occasionally experiences the difficulty of describing Congolese life in French as evinced by his retention of African words for objects which do not exist in France and have, therefore, no French equivalent: *pagnes, saca-saca, ndumba*. His dilemma will be magnified by our translation of the text into another language yet one step further removed from the society he describes.

Just those aspects of Lopes' writing which make his work accessible to a wide audience in French – his clarity, his simplicity, the detail in which he writes, his universality – also tend to make his work translatable. His stories are not overly culture-bound; they speak of a foreign culture but in a modern, familiar way.

Since Lopes' original title, *Tribaliques*, relates so explicitly to his entire philosophy, the translator felt it was critical to retain the allusion to tribalism and translate it as closely as possible. *Tribaliks* keeps the tribal reference yet being a construct (as is 'tribaliques'), puts the reader on guard that something unexpected is spoken of inside the cover. They will not find the African bush or black Africans oppressed by white colonialization but rather modern, urban Africa with all its inherent social problems.

Lopes writes with an alteration of short declarative sentences (even sentence fragments), and longer, complex ones. In many instances his rhythm could be maintained in translation and still produce easily flowing English prose. At other times, short sentences of his were combined to form a longer one in English, or longer sentences were divided up. On the whole, the translation attempts to maintain a balance similar to that of the French text.

It is worth noting two unusual elements of the author's otherwise straightforward style which are evident already in the short stories and become expanded in his novels. The point of view from which the story is told shifts back and forth, making for a structural complexity even within a single paragraph. A passage may start with the thoughts of the character and shift into the narrator's comments. This develops into epistolary interludes in *La Nouvelle Romance*.

Lopes also employs time and verb tenses in a very fluid manner, perhaps reminiscent of the shifts in tenses used during traditional oral storytelling. The translation occasionally maintained this fluidity in instances when it did not cause undue confusion in the story line. When a choice was called for between literal tense usage and a clear narrative, clarity was chosen over fidelity.

Henri Lopes speaks of a new era of African literature, one in which the major problem is no longer whether to maintain traditional structures in the face of European colonization but rather how Africans can adapt to a society which is in the process of rapid evolution. He views all oppressed peoples, no matter their skin colour, as fighting a common enemy. Just as he places the oppression of African women into the context of world-wide women's liberation, so for him does the political corruption in contemporary Africa reflect the larger problem of equality and justice for all humankind. In this sense Lopes' ideology can be considered revolutionary despite his strong pro-Western stance and his important governmental positions.

Henri Lopes' message is one that is sure to interest Western readers. His voice deserves to be heard outside Africa. It is the translator's hope that the present volume succeeds in its attempts to reproduce faithfully both Lopes' message and his voice, as it introduces the English-language public to an interesting and important literary figure from contemporary Africa.

A.L.

1   Alexandre Mboukou, 'US/Congo: Pragmatic Relations', *Africa Report*, 26, No. 6 (Nov–Dec 1981), 14.
2   Mboukou, 14.
3   Mboukou, 17.
4   Claude S. Phillips, *The African Political Dictionary*, (ABC-CLIO Info. Services, Santa Barbara, Calif. 1984), p. 32.

5   Chief Emeka Anyaoku, 'Changing Attitudes: A Coopera-
     tive Effort', *Africa Report*, 30, No. 2 (March–April 1985),
     21.

6   Henri Lopes, 'Préface', *Emancipation féminine et roman
     africain*, by Arlette Chemain–Degrange, (Nouvelles
     Éditions Africaines, Dakar, 1979), p. 11.

7   Rose Francine Rogombe, 'Equal Partners in Africa's
     Development', *Africa Report*, 30, No. 2 (March–April
     1985), 19.

8   Rogombe, 20.

9   Anyaoku, 22.

10   Rogombe, 20.

11   Jacques Chevrier, 'Écriture noire en ques-
     tion', Notre Librairie, 65, (July–Sept. 1982), 16.

12   Henri Lopes, address presented to the African Literature
     Association, Ithaca, N.Y., 11 April 1987.

13   Balliet Bleziri Camille, 'Recontre avec Henri Lopes,
     écrivain', *Bingo*, (Jan 1977), p. 59.

14   Frédéric Grah Mel, 'Henri Lopes: L'écrivain doit
     prendre position, ou se taire', Fraternité Matin, 26
     Oct. 1976, 17.

15   George Steiner, 'Introduction' to *The Penguin Book of
     Modern Verse Translation*, ed. G. S. (Penguin Books,
     Harmondsworth, 1966), p. 23.

EXODUS OF THE SKILLED WORKERS

Seated in the taxi driving from Maya-Maya to his home, Mbouloukoué watched Brazzaville awaken. The streets were mostly deserted. Several women, empty baskets on their heads, made their way to market. Here and there a man on a bicycle, probably a houseboy, pedalled his way to work. It was 5.30 a.m. The morning air was cool, yet to Mbouloukoué it felt more oppressive than the air he had been breathing in Europe just a few hours earlier. His taxi approached the area of the city near the General Hospital. All the windows were still closed.

Mbouloukoué had not slept the previous night. He never could sleep on aeroplanes. Yet he did not feel tired that morning. He was preoccupied with the thought of how he would break the news to Mbâ. It was Sunday and he did not want to arrive at her home too early. To help pass the time, he busied himself, undressed, showered and dressed again in lightweight clothes. Then he unpacked his bags and set aside a package Elo had given him for Mbâ.

Mbouloukoué walked towards the post office and stopped at a nearby bakery for breakfast. After eating, he called 28–72. From the sound of her voice, he could tell that Mbâ was already up.

'Oh, it's you, Mbouloukoué. Are you back already?'

'Yes, I just got in.'

'And?'

1

She wanted to know everything right away. What could he say?

'I have a gift for you from Elo. May I come around?'

'Of course. Come right over.'

Mbâ, Elo and Mbouloukoué were all born in the village of Ossio. They went to school together every morning, crossing the Nkeni River and walking many miles to reach Ngamboma. After graduating from the local school the same year, they all moved to Brazzaville where their strong bonds of friendship were really forged. They used to get together and talk about their studies.

Mbâ had loved both Elo and Mbouloukoué, equally, as brothers. She thought Mbouloukoué was the handsomer of the two, and he, when he looked at her or spoke to her alone, found something different in her, something the other girls lacked. These young women, Mbâ's colleagues at school, seemed uninterested in what they were learning. They went to class every day as if going to a party. They took great pains with their clothes and carried their books so as to be noticed by the men they passed in the streets. School was the place to meet their girlfriends, with whom they exchanged romance magazines featuring the type of story in which a man was loved by two women. The less likeable of the two would finally reveal her selfish intentions, or discover that she in turn was loved by another man better suited to her.

The girls discussed the price of make-up and hairdos, and exchanged tips on where to go for bargains on clothes, make-your-skin-soft-as-silk soap or wigs from Kinshasa. All this was done to impress the high level officials and military officers who met them when school finished to make dates, or simply to take them for a 'spin along the Northern road' in flashy cars. Some of the girls even bragged of having a child by Mr So-and-So, president of such and such a company. Others took to offering candles and prayers to Saint Anne, or giving money to a well-known crippled fetishist thus enlisting his help in catching those attractive executives who, despite their good looks, were loyal to their wives and did not date other women. Several of the girls wanted to get a piece of that cake too.

Mbâ avoided these groups. She was too acutely aware of the sacrifices her family was making to send her to school. Everything taught in class interested her. Once she was enthralled when a physics teacher, obliged to chastise a student for her failure to give in homework, digressed and spoke at length about Marie Curie. Another time, Mbâ was fascinated by a female character in a novel she discovered at the library. She even memorized the last paragraph:

'Here begins modern romance. Here ends the story of chivalry. Here for the first time a place has been made for true love, love which is not tarnished by the supremacy of man over woman, by the sordid preoccupation with dresses and kisses, by the domination of man's money over woman, or of woman over man. Modern woman is born, and it is of her I sing. And of her I shall sing.'

Mbâ's conversation with Mbouloukoué and Elo always revealed her reactions to what she had seen. The three young people unendingly exchanged opinions about everyday life around them. They were disgusted by life in Brazzaville, and recalled with emotion a certain man they had known in Ossio whom they still considered to be a symbol of moral virtue.

They enjoyed attending local Party meetings, branches of which had been newly established in several areas of the city. At their branch, they especially enjoyed listening to a young student, recently returned from France, who spoke of men called Marx, Engels, Lenin and Mao Tse Tung (a Chinese apparently). It was all very inspiring and beautiful, like a breath of fresh air wafting over old Batéké Street, foretelling the coming of a better world.

Mbouloukoué frequented the embassies of the socialist countries and brought back publications which the friends exchanged and discussed, and over which they dreamed. This

3

was one year after the revolution.* Everyone spoke of scientific socialism. Elo thought it was the only worthwhile future, but expressed a lack of confidence in the honesty of the individuals who touted its virtues most often.

Mbâ was preoccupied with the situation of women and wanted to devote herself to their cause. She doubted that city women were in any position to help their sisters. The married women were too intimidated to go out and become activists. In the evenings their husbands held them accountable for their daytime hours. As for the most visible militant feminists, they were really no more than pleasant, high class prostitutes, 'ndumba', literate but unwilling to fight for an end to polygamy. Rather they mocked the married women who hoped to keep their husbands to themselves. In Mbâ's eyes they were undeserving of emancipation. Emancipation, on the other hand, had a meaning for women like her mother who walked six miles a day back and forth to the plantation to work the land; women who carried on their backs baskets weighing up to a hundred pounds, and whose foreheads were permanently marked by the carrying straps. Many men, after a quarter of a mile, would have collapsed under such a load. While the women worked the fields, the men stayed in the village, in the shade, talking or sleeping, with a bottle of the bamboo wine, molengué, within easy reach. But the women who occupied Mbá's thoughts were illiterate, unable to read or write, incapable of ordering their thoughts. They would be afraid to talk into a microphone. It was unthinkable to send them abroad as representatives to speak out about the problems of women. For the moment they must resign themselves to work, suffer, age prematurely, and let the ndumba play the role of spokeswomen for African women's emancipation.

*The 13th, 14th and 15th of August 1963, known as 'The Three Glorious Days', when President Youlou was overthrown and a one-party state established which later adopted scientific socialism as its national ideology.

4

All this intrigued Mbouloukoué, but he never admitted it to Mbâ. He realized only too well that she listened more willingly to Elo. Elo loved soccer and Mbâ always enjoyed accompanying him to the games, where he would cheer enthusiastically for the local team.

One evening, on the way home from a game at the Eboué stadium, a storm caught Elo and Mbâ by surprise. They had just enough time to take cover. Mbâ complained of how her hair was soaked, and after she had just that morning unbraided it. Elo's shirt was dripping wet. He took it off. Each time it thundered, Mbâ involuntarily huddled against him. They were alone under the tree at the bus station. Elo was aware of Mbâ's body under her clinging, wet dress. He shuddered, and pulled her to him. She closed her eyes, snuggled against him and sighed. They held each other tight.

When the rain stopped at eleven o'clock, Mbâ did not return to Mama Nguélélé's house where she was lodging. Although surprised to see her niece return home at six in the morning, the old woman asked no questions.

After this, the relationship among the three friends continued as before. Mbâ and Elo kept their evening meetings secret from Mbouloukoué. He wouldn't have been jealous, but Mbâ and Elo did not want him to feel in the way. He seemed unaware, and only noticed that Mbâ behaved differently. It seemed as if her hips were looser. A previously nonexistent light gleamed in her eyes.

Then came exam period. Mbouloukoué, always first in his class, was accepted at university to continue his studies. Mbâ took the qualifying exams for entrance into the Teacher's Training College in Mouyondzi. She wanted to help her family, especially her younger brothers and sisters, as soon as possible.

Elo received his certificate as a licensed welder. He was hired at a factory at Mpila. One day he learned of a government sponsored competition to select three welders who would be sent to France for further training. Elo applied

5

and was chosen. He would be gone for two years. He sent Mbâ a telegram and she arranged to spend a couple of days in Brazzaville. The young people loved each other with a greater fervour and passion than ever before. They spent two intense days and nights filled with sighs, smiles and pleasures, despite the tears that Mbâ could not control when she thought of how Elo was being taken away from her. He gave her a gold necklace, purchased from a Senegalese merchant with the first instalment of his stipend.

After Elo's departure, Mbâ at first received one letter a week from him, full of his longing for her. Then his unhappiness ceased, and he described all he discovered in France and how life was so much easier there. Two months went by without a letter. Finally he wrote no more. After two years, Mbâ learned from Elo's friends that he was working at a factory in Nantes.

Now, six years later, Elo still has not returned. Mbâ works at a school in Bacongo. She is an excellent teacher, popular with both parents and students. This is partially because students enjoy having an attractive teacher, but also because she is skilled. Often the youngest of her colleagues ask her out, but she always declines. She socializes so rarely, it is difficult for men to even meet her. Each evening after class, she teaches illiterate adults. Some of her adult women students have become friends. Mbâ learns from them in exchange. She has confided in Mbouloukoué her plans to write a book about Congolese women based on this experience.

Mbouloukoué is a teacher at Kinkala. He too is unmarried. He devotes all his time to studying and teaching mathematics and to directing the local youth organization.

One Saturday, Mbouloukoué came to Brazzaville to see Mbâ and tell her he had just been chosen as a delegate to a meeting in France on teaching modern mathematics. Together they tried to contact Elo's classmates to get his address. Mbâ bought dried fish, *foufou* flour, okra and two pineapples which she entrusted to Mbouloukoué as a gift for Elo, the one she was waiting for, the one who had gone away. She did not even stop to think that France was a large country and that Elo might not get to meet their childhood friend. Mbâ told Mbouloukoué everything he should say to Elo. What she could not tell him, she wrote in a long, ten-page letter that Mbouloukoué was to deliver.

***

In Paris, with the help of Ebon, a mutual friend, Mbouloukoué learned the name of the factory where Elo worked. And so, one Friday afternoon, after adventures that would not interest the reader, Elo and Mbouloukoué walked together along Quai de la Fosse in Nantes. They talked, slapping each other on the shoulder every few seconds. Finally they took a bus to the suburb where Elo lived.

'Come with me, brother. I have a few errands to run on the way home. In this country, even we men have to lend a hand in running the house.'

Mbouloukoué was astonished to see Elo enter a grocery store and buy milk, butter and fruit, stop at the bakery for bread and at the butcher's shop (after having asked Mbouloukoué what he would like) for steak. They then went to a tobacconist where Elo bought a package of Gauloises cigarettes and the evening paper, *France-Soir*, so he could bet on the horses.

'You know, I have to do some of the shopping. My wife comes home too late.'

'Your wife?'

'Didn't you know? I'm married, old man.'

Mbouloukoué was struck dumb. In all honesty, to express what he really felt, he should have shouted at Elo, even punched him in the face. He wanted to call him a dirty bastard, deny his friendship and threaten to leave by the first train … Instead he only stopped dead in his tracks. They were climbing the stairs so he could look Elo right in the eyes, coldly and contemptuously. He thought of Mbâ, so beautiful, so

7

desirable. Mbâ at home, who had been leading a life of seclusion for several years.

'And Mbâ?'

'Come on in. I'll explain it all to you.'

Elo, as charming and smooth-spoken as ever, talked about his loneliness in France. He spoke of Hélène (his wife) and how she had helped him. He spoke of their son.

'So, I don't think I'll be going back home. Here a skilled worker isn't a millionaire but he can still live better than an educated government employee at home. I've checked it out. At home in my line of work I could earn 30.000 CFA francs*. Here I earn three times that with twice the buying power. My dear friend, since you have connections with the authorities, let them know how things are. If they're not careful, there won't be just a brain-drain but an exodus of the skilled workers as well.'

'What about your family?'

'One day, if I manage to save up enough money, we'll go back and visit. For the moment, it's out of the question. I know how things are at home, anything left over from my earnings would go to feed nephews and nieces, children of do-nothing so-called cousins. And as you know, old man, I'd have to accept another wife; get married in the traditional way. Hélène wouldn't stand for that.

***

Mbâ heard the knock on the door. She ran to open it. Mbouloukoué was standing there, his face drawn as if announcing a death.

Dear God, what can he say to her?

---

*Currency of the French African Community. 488 CFA francs = approximately £1.00

OH, APOLLINE

I can still see myself in Father Flandrin's study.

'My dear Raphael, is there no way to keep you? All I can ask you, my son, is to remain true to the teaching you have received here. The Church is more than just those who wear the habit. We also need lay people to help disseminate the faith. I am confident you will spread about your love of Our Saviour, the Lord Jesus.'

As I listened to him, I almost changed my mind. I could just picture throwing myself sobbing into his arms. The theatricality of the act is what most probably stopped me.

That meeting with Father Flandrin reawakened in me the almost physical pleasure I derived from his philosophy courses. He did not preach doctrine, nor provide a weapon, a recipe, for defending our faith in the face of life's trials. Rather he helped us to discover the meaning of human existence, and the possibility of logic and love working in partnership for a world of happiness and brotherhood. Father Flandrin spoke to us of everything, including Marxism and sex. Nothing was taboo. He would begin each discussion by presenting the most atheistic viewpoint, arguing in its favour with such unassailable logic that we asked ourselves if he were not really partisan to this philosophy so diametrically opposed to the Church's beliefs, to be able to dispose of the latter so easily and satirically. Then we would attack the atheistic position which he so deftly defended against our arguments as to make us feel they were half-baked and unsophisticated. When we were defeated and about to concede, ready to accuse him of being an unbeliever, he would draw on his arsenal of noble and lofty criticisms, and in his elegant way refute the atheistic philosophy. This done, he would then present a point of view less diametrically opposed to the one we would finally accept, the one held by the Church. Thus gradually, progressively, he would lead us towards the Teilhardian ideal where scientific inquiry, progress, and faith harmonize perfectly.

He did not hestitate to employ atheistic or Marxist terminology in order to defend the Christian position. Even today when I meet my seminary colleagues, no matter which direction their lives have taken, I clearly recognize the familiar mental cast, fruit of the seed planted by Father Flandrin: rejection of dogmatism, folly, and hatred, coupled with an unshakable faith in a doctrine far removed from the eclectic. Whether they be Marxists or missionaries, Father Flandrin's students share a common brotherhood.

While the priest was discussing my departure, I was overcome with nostalgia for the intellectually challenging experiences which I had so much enjoyed. It was the honesty he had strengthened in me that reinforced my decision to leave. But I was also sensing a fear of committing myself to a life in which he would no longer be available to answer my questions. Because I have forgotten to mention that whenever any doubts formed in our minds following a lecture or caused by an unexpected situation, we would call on Father Flandrin at his study in the evening. He would help us to see just how simple the problem actually was and where the obvious solution lay. He followed us with the reasoning of Columbus with the egg. The answer was self-evident if we just opened our eyes.

I did not, however, revoke my decision. For better or worse, I no longer subscribed to those beliefs which originally drove me into the seminary. I had just lived through two years of intense, sometimes painful internal debate which convinced me I was not cut out for what we called carnal abstinence, and that further, the celibacy of priests was as unnatural as certain physical mutilations of our ancient traditional religious rituals.

10

How could one possibly promise never to share physical love with a woman? Even the most upright and self-possessed priest – at the end of a good meal accompanied by those fine wines which Europe has taught us to appreciate, under the ecstatic spell of a sea-blue sky shrieking with colour and flooded with sunlight – even the most morally pure priest could not help but desire the beautiful, well-built young woman who passed by. As for me, frequent nightly profanations had convinced me I was obsessed with the problem. I even – and why not admit it – even succumbed occasionally to masturbation.

I knew that upon leaving the seminary I would be facing great challenges. As regards my studies, that is. Because the new direction I had chosen for my life was the narrow perspective of academic success. During the vacation which followed my departure from the seminary, I prepared myself not only for the work ahead, which would require a great deal of reading in a variety of subjects, but also for the self-discipline I would have to practise until receiving my degree.

From what I saw around me I concluded that the young people were distracted from their studies by two diversions: sports and women. I already knew that most Congolese students had such a passion for the former it seemed as if their studies were the relaxation and not the contrary. They were content to attend classes regularly and memorize whatever nonsense the teacher spouted forth from his rostrum. Only a handful would read supplementary material, either for greater understanding or to refute the ideas of the professor. Samba Jones, my room mate on the Quinze-Ans Plateau, complained that our scholarships were too meagre to pay for our books. Yet we were earning twice the wages of a worker in a textile factory. Having been accustomed to no pocket money at all in the seminary, I felt rich and therefore uneasy. If I remarked to Samba that the sports magazines he bought and which filled his room, the games he always attended, his sports equipment, and the dues he paid to support the Djoué Tornados cost him more than the books I bought, he just shrugged. And all my classmates were the same. They passionately loved soccer and looked on their studies as merely a means to acquire the credentials necessary to insure a certain standard of living.

As for women, who could avoid them? They charmed, turned childhood friends into enemies, swallowed up fellow-ship money – in brief preoccupied the student body in one form or another twenty-four hours a day. I do not mean just the few *ndumba**. Some students had a wife (others two or three) and children to support on their limited fellowships. But a certain self-knowledge made me especially uneasy. I am the sort of person who cannot dedicate himself to more than one thing at a time. I live everything passionately. And if I were to fall in love with a woman, my studies would suffer. I would no longer take them seriously. Yet it was important to me to show my colleagues from the seminary that although I had given up the frock I had not rejected a serious view of life, that my conception of the world did not exclude a certain renunciation. So I decided to leave women alone and devote myself to my studies. To tell the truth, I did not rule out some brief and discreet one-time encounters. But for this I knew I would have to avoid the young women of my age and profit from the fleeting desires of a mature woman, possibly married, and preferably from another region and only passing through Brazzaville.

From the very beginning of the school year, I attacked my studies with a zeal that frightened Samba. He studied at the library no more than one hour each week and spent an inordinate amount of time discussing what seemed to me only idle chatter of a very superficial nature. He called it contact with the masses and formation of a political consciousness. Samba did have a few books on the shelf above his bed. A volume of Senghor's poetry I believe, a pocket edition of St Exupéry, and the books *How to Interpret Dreams*, *Everything You Need to Know About the Stars*, and *How to Become a Successful Public*

*Luxury call girl without procurer.

12

Speaker. These surrounded Mao's '*little red book*' and two volumes covered in chocolate brown on which were printed in gold letters the name 'Lenin'. I don't know when he glanced through or read them. It was more a decoration, like the photo of the Bantou orchestra that hung on the wall. Because Samba loved music. Whenever he was alone, the record player or radio would blare the currently popular songs, while Samba, in front of the mirror, would practise the *yéké-yéké*, rocking nimbly from one leg to another, moving forwards and backwards like a walking camel. My study habits certainly frightened Samba, and most probably he would have looked for another room mate if we had not been from the same village. But we Congolese still believe that family ties and a common dialect are stronger than common interests.

As for me, I had found a work rhythm which made my days seem too short. As soon as classes were over, I rushed to the library or some other place where I was sure not to be disturbed.

One day, a month after classes had begun, Samba announced that he and some classmates were giving a party the following Saturday. It would not cost us a cent. The others would supply the drinks and bring the girls. We would only have to provide the locale and the music.

My immediate and strong negative reaction startled my friend. He advised me to relax a little or else I would get prematurely grey. We talked for nearly an hour. What we said is not worth repeating. He did not convince me, but did force a wedge into my defences and start me thinking. The following days I constantly reworked our discussion in my mind. I found myself stopped by such frivolous and trivial arguments as: 'One must relax and have fun. It's only normal.' The following moment I would regain control and tell myself that a good book is a far superior way to relax than dancing, and that Africa, by laughing and singing, had let sterner, more austere people take her by surprise, and subjugate and deport her people. Each evening we spent dancing at Poto-Poto, scholars, strategists, and the military were studying and

13

training in the south of our continent to increase our enslavement. What will we do the day they arrive at our borders? Will we be able to disarm them with the charm of our voices and our songs? Will our music stop them? Will they join us in dancing to the rhythm of a well-played conga? And I wondered if the few Chinese experts who had just arrived in the country to help us with some economic projects took us seriously or if, deep inside, they laughed at men who cried Marx louder than the Red Guard but who could not give up even the most idle of pastimes.

Nonetheless, on Saturday evening I found myself alongside Samba receiving our guests.

I had been caught up in the preparations. In the morning, I had helped Samba borrow chairs from our neighbours and even from a local bar which also agreed to lend us glasses. I spent the entire afternoon wiring the record player and the two loud speakers so they would play stereo. Samba also wanted special lighting effects which varied with the music's rhythm. It was magical for him. It was fun for me, so I set about trying to create what he wanted.

No doubt it was the preparations of the party that caught me up. Also, Samba needed my help.

Early in the evening I took on the role of host. I prepared drinks and served them. I took charge of changing the records and arranging the lighting. When I had a free moment, I sat and watched the couples dancing. Normally I thought dancers looked ridiculous. That Saturday evening, the two glasses of whiskey I had downed helped me appreciate and follow their movements. In surprise I sometimes caught myself clapping hands and rocking my head, or swinging my body from side to side in time to the music I was humming. Almost automatically my eyes fell on a girl I had seen several times at school. While all the other girls at the party were wearing wigs – some enormous, some curly – her hair was short, cut like a man's. It added a natural touch to her beauty. She was tall and thin, but well-built. There was something regal in her beauty. I felt that one could not ask such a girl to become a lover, only a wife. And it was evident from her way of smiling, from her expression, that she was the intellectual equal of any of the young men there. I wanted to ask her to dance but could not gather my courage. I feared my strong desire would betray itself on my face and, if I asked her to dance, she would see it and make fun of me and my immodest feelings. Whereas she, despite the sensuality of her beauty, inspired only pure and decent love. I was sure such beauty was obvious to other eyes than mine. Since I was trying to find out which of my fellow students was her steady date at the moment, I hesitated to approach her. Could she possibly be 'unattached'? Was she a beauty whose head had not been turned by her good looks and who thought she had more serious work to do for the moment than just play at love? Love would come afterwards. Although such girls were rare, there was a growing number of women who had more ambition than the majority of the young men. If such were the case, I would wish to meet her in two, three or four years. But I would be taking a chance, waiting so long and then hopefully arriving at just the right moment.

Everyone in the room was standing, dancing the 'jerk' with machine-like movements. I marvelled at how each dancer played with the rhythm. James Brown belted out that he was black and proud of it. That he felt great. The dancers' responses to the music were reminiscent of the interaction between our traditional musicians and a crowd of villagers. When the music stopped, everyone clapped. Samba was delighted with the ambiance. His guests no longer danced to impress their partners but purely for their own pleasure. I think it was then, if I remember correctly, that I put on an Afro-Cuban number, 'Marinero'. As soon as I heard the first few notes, I recognized the tune as one to which my parents liked to dance when I was a child, a dance called the G.V. Everyone clapped. The beautiful girl approached me.

'You're not dancing, comrade. Come on. Dance with me.'

I did not even stop to think whether or not I knew the steps. I would manage well enough. Better not disappoint her. And

15

so I danced, we danced. Has a Congolese woman ever been your partner for a rumba? If so, you need no further explanation. If not, imagine her hips rolling like waves, moving to the music, carrying you on and on.

But you must know that the rumba can really only be danced well when the partners are pressed tightly together. And we danced well. We did not say a word while the music was playing. But I think dancers speak with their bodies.

When the record ended, Jonas quickly put it on again. I blessed him silently and took my partner in my arms again.

'You're at the University, aren't you?' she asked me.

'Yes.'

'But I don't see you often.'

'I have a lot of work.'

Our conversation stopped there but we both felt we had a great deal more to say to each other. And at the time, I didn't know how to speak to girls. I ever-so-slightly raised my hand which was on her back, and touched her skin just above the neckline. She did not stiffen at the contact. I even had the impression that she pressed imperceptibly closer to me. With my other hand I squeezed her thumb. She returned the gesture by holding my hand tighter. We finished the dance cheek to cheek.

For the remainder of the evening, as soon as I heard the notes of a song, even before I could tell if it was something I knew, I asked her to dance. Of course, a few times friends beat me to it. I noticed she did not dance quite so close with the others. But whenever she was with someone else, I fumed with jealousy and forced my face into a mask which hid my true feelings. Because, after all, maybe she had only pressed my hand from nervousness. If so, she would be annoyed to see my jealousy. To be legitimately jealous, one has to have been granted certain rights. And I thought at the time that serious girls preferred to hide their true feelings at first. Therefore, I had to respect her feminine modesty.

There were also times during the evening when she did not dance. I stayed beside her to talk. Her name was Apolline and she was in her second year, studying English. She wanted to become an interpreter, if only she could win a fellowship to study abroad the following year. Then we spoke about some professors and our impressions of their teaching. We also discussed the poverty of our cultural life in Brazzaville and, without realizing it, passed on to our views on the theatre and Black African writers. Several times I surprised myself by my 'sin of self-pride', as we called it in the seminary. In order to shine for Apolline, I occasionally defended points of view which I had only partially understood, citing to support my ideas authors I had not always read. I experienced a drunkenness, sweeter than any which could have been due to the drinks I had imbibed earlier in the evening. Since my departure from the seminary, this was the first time I had engaged in a discussion at such a level. The rare instances when I had wanted to exchange opinions with my colleagues, I was shocked by the weakness of their arguments. Like idlers who not knowing what to do with their hands use them to throw rocks at passers-by, the minds and tongues of my colleagues were especially dexterous at tearing apart their neighbours. Such was not the case with Apolline.

At one point, when our conversation lapsed for several minutes, she glanced at my watch.

'It's getting late. I must be going now.'

'But the party is at its best.'

'Yes, exactly. I prefer to leave with this memory rather than wait until the end when it all peters out and everyone is exhausted. You know,' she said, 'a good time is like a piece of sugar cane. Once you have sucked out all the juice and chewed out the sugar, it's not worth keeping in your mouth. You only get the taste of the tough, coarse fibre and uselessly tire your jaws.'

'May I walk you home?'

She didn't answer, but I glimpsed in her eyes a passing gleam of pleasure as if she had tasted some good, iced palm wine. Her silence made me uncomfortable. She closed her eyes and moved only her lips.

'Why not?'

She lived close by. Outside, I was at a loss for words. I really wanted to declare my love for her already but feared she might just laugh in my face. Should I take her hand, her arm, or hold her around the waist? Our hands were not far apart. I have already described how we had squeezed them while dancing and how our bodies had been pressed together. Why was I so paralysed, why couldn't I carry out the same movements which had been so natural in public just a moment earlier? It was only when I saw we were nearing her street that I decided to put my arm around her and pull her towards me.

'Apolline, I want to kiss you.'

I had seen in films that the first commitment of a woman to a man was a kiss on the lips. She put her head on my chest and instead of offering me her lips, she pressed herself against me. I heard her sigh. There, I had done it! I had annoyed her. But by then I had gone so far I could not turn back.

'Do you find me so unattractive?'

She pressed even more strongly against me and sighed again. I understood less and less. I was just about to let her go, to give up, when I realized she did not want to let go of me.

'You're not making fun of me?', she asked with a childlike voice, looking at me straight in the eyes.

I shook my head. She began to cry.

***

When I returned to the party I wanted to jump about and cry out. I had a girl friend. I was loved.

***

We agreed to meet the following day and I took her out along the road at the northern end of the city, into a valley which had been developed by an aged mulatto. Surrounding the artificial lake he had created were straw huts serving local dishes: *malangua* in *liboké*, *saca-saca*, chicken *batéké* with *pili-pili*, *manioc*. Children played with dug-outs on the lake.

Apolline confessed she would like to go out in a boat, but we both agreed we would prefer a more private place. It would have been exhibitionism there since the huts around the lake were like the grandstand around a stadium.

This time we spoke of different things than on the previous night. We wanted to get to know each other. I learned some of her secrets. She had been engaged once, to a childhood friend, but had broken it off the year before.

'He was very handsome.'

They had been together for a while at secondary school. Then he left. One day he returned, back from the Congo-Kinshasa. Now a diamond merchant, he was rolling in money and drove a Mercedes convertible.

At first he lavished attention on her, but later became nasty.

'What do you mean by nasty?'

'Oh, you know,' she said, shrugging.

I confided in her too. I told her about my childhood. How at a tender age, by entering first the juvenate and then the seminary, I had cut myself off from contact with the world. I told her of my hopes and fears. Today when I think back on it, I cannot help smiling. I tried to paint myself as a mysterious romantic, misunderstood by my family, society and friends. She was the first person who seemed to understand me. There had, of course, been Father Flandrin. But he was my superior, whom I admired and who renewed hope in the existence of some basic good in mankind. But there were certain things I had never been able to tell him.

'At times I consider writing about it. I think I have lived through enough personal experiences to make a novel.'

'Why don't you write?'

'My studies, exams …'

She took hold of my hands and looked into my eyes.

'But don't you know, writing is more important than your studies.'

When we arrived back in Brazzaville, we didn't know where to go. The streets are all deserted on Sunday. For people who don't frequent bars or enjoy engaging in useless chatter, there is not much to do. There are, of course, cinemas with their westerns or American detective films of questionable taste. One can also jump about and get worked up at the Revolutionary Stadium, rooting for one team or another. But Apolline shared my complete condemnation of these pastimes. That day, however, we blessed sports. Since Jonas had gone to cheer for the Djoué Tornados, the house was empty and Apolline could accompany me home without embarrassment.

When we found ourselves alone, my timidity of the previous evening reappeared.

But, oh, how sweet it was! I can still see her under me, eyes closed, cheek against the pillow, breathing heavily.

When I awoke, she looked at me and with a finger, traced my eyebrows, my nose, my lips.

'Sleep,' she whispered.

I closed my eyes and smiled at her.

'You know, my fiancé really was handsome.'

I began to wonder about that fiancé, who always seemed to come between us. I wanted her to describe him completely. Although I didn't wish to imitate him, I hoped that by knowing his qualities I could guess the circumstances in which Apolline would be led to compare us.

She confided that she had loved him so very much that finally she could no longer do without him. They decided to get married the following year. In the meantime, they lived together. At first it was like a honeymoon. Then, while she stayed at home studying in the evening, he started going out without her. He never told her where, nor with whom. Of course, Apolline knew the customs of Congolese men, yet she could not get used to it. At first she tried to overcome her jealousy. But how could she sleep peacefully when he didn't return before five or seven in the morning? If she said anything, he answered rudely that women should mind their own business and keep their noses out of their husband's affairs. When her older sister visited her in Brazzaville, Apolline complained to her in the hope that she would somehow manage to change things. Her sister sighed and said:

'What do you expect me to do? That's the way things are. We can't change them. When I was first married, I couldn't stand it either. But as time passed – well – I've got used to it. He's a man, you're a woman. Each sex has its own rights. Now when I get the chance to have some fun without my husband finding out, I don't hesitate.

It consoles me. As for you, what you should think about is his money.

Apolline tried everything: gentleness, anger, visits to the fetishist. At times her fiancé would be faithful for a whole week. Then he would spend every night for two weeks away from home. Sometimes he would only return to eat at noon for half an hour, and then go off again. While he was away, she would get anonymous phone calls:

'Is that Apolline?'

'Yes.'

'You'd be better off leaving home. Your beloved Albert is here with me right now. I've satisfied him so well that he's sleeping just beside me.'

And when she asked Albert about it, he always denied everything. Finally she got fed up and left.

Apolline always compared me to her former fiancé. In my opinion so stunning a girl, with such a special personality and unusual level of awareness, was an exceptional thing in our country. And to think she loved me made my head spin. Little by little I lost control of myself. But women are strange. Why had she ever loved this diamond merchant who seemed so vulgar?

I devoted less and less time to my studies and spent more time in Apolline's arms, in her bed or in mine. When I reacted and mentioned my work, she mocked me and said that at this rate I would wear myself out. With all I already knew why did I still have to learn more? I had heard similar remarks before but had never paid any attention to them, knowing full well that in the near future a new generation would arise, more aware of its responsibilities and harder working than any of us. Yet it was sufficient for the words to come from her mouth to awaken in me a feeling of self-satisfaction. Upon leaving the seminary, I had not been certain that what I had learned there would be any use to me at the university. Apolline assured me I was well-above average. And as it came from her, I believed it.

Sometimes Apolline teased me.

'Hey, black man, I don't like the way that girl looked at you!'

'Which girl?'

'Don't act so innocent! Don't put on that serious look when you're really hiding a smirk. You know full well which girl I mean!'

'No I don't.'

'Oh, I want to pinch or bite you.' And she bit me.

After a moment she calmed down and said:

'Just remember you belong to me. I'll scratch out the eyes of any girl who dares touch you.'

Of course there was a touch of flirtation in all this. But I had noticed that since I was dating Apolline, other women, beautiful women, looked enviously at us. Often women don't desire a man until he is shown off by another woman.

But I will quickly bore you if I recount all the things that made up our relationship. I don't know if it's really true that happy couples have no story to tell. But I do know their stories irritate those who listen to or read them.

The days flew by because I thought only of making the moments together with Apolline last as long as possible. She was the one, while pulling out of an embrace, who reminded me that the Christmas vacation was fast approaching.

'I want you to come with me to Mossaka*. I'm sure my parents will like you. I don't want us to be separated, not even for two weeks.'

I wondered if she were serious, and finally convinced myself she was accustomed to more spontaneity with her parents than I was with mine. It must have been the custom of her tribe.

To win his beloved, a man must vanquish his shyness, be

*A city approximately 300 miles inland, up the Congo River from Brazzaville.

brave enough to take her hand and stand completely naked, as it were, before her, even the first time. He cannot be afraid to meet her parents.

This time, however, I could not control myself. I was afraid to visit people of another tribe who, if one thinks about it, might have imagined a totally different future for their daughter. And since our numerous dates and all the little gifts I had given her left me penniless at the end of the month, not only would I be unable to offer her family the traditional gifts expected by future-in-laws, but I would not even have enough money to pay my boat fare to Mossaka.

The day she left, I accompanied her to the dock. We felt ourselves totally separate from the noisy crowd around us – people talking and carrying baskets full of *manioc* and other objects bought in the city. Most of the travellers were preoccupied with finding a comfortable seat. Several of them, acquaintances of Apolline, interrupted us to talk with her. They were from her region of the country and spoke in their dialect. I was annoyed because I couldn't understand what they said. Although I was unsure how I would feel when the boat actually left, I was still eager for it to depart. The last few minutes before a separation are always difficult ones.

There was nothing more to add to all I had been telling her since the previous day, yet I could not bring myself to leave. When the moment to say goodbye finally arrived, she stepped up onto the two boards that served as a gangplank. Her eyes clouded with tears and she said, smiling:

'Tell me, my big black man, do you think I'll return?'

And while the boat moved off towards the Mbamou Island, her words continued to ring in my ears.

***

Classes had resumed almost ten days earlier. Apolline had not returned nor had I received the telegram she promised to send so I could meet her.

I knew the boat made the trip irregularly, only twice a month or so. After class I went to the dock for information. I was told the boat from Mossaka was scheduled to arrive in two

23

days at about 7.30 a.m. but that the time was only approximate since it often ran several hours late. My heart skipped a beat. I was unable to live without Apolline. Ever since her departure the world had seemed dull. I spent much of my time searching for a present to give her. Most lovers instinctively find some personal gift especially pleasing to the beloved. But I had noticed Apolline's unusual and refined taste, so was afraid of choosing something she would not like. Also women's clothing and jewellery are far too expensive for a student who must help support his family with his fellowship. I borrowed Samba's motor bike and rode to the studio of a sculptor I knew who lived along the road north of the city. He had moved there to escape from both the crowds and his family in Poto-Poto who did not understand that artistic creation is a serious pursuit and requires continuous, solitary work. I explained my reason for coming. He helped me choose a piece and only let me pay half price for it. I selected a mask.

When the day came, I was at the harbour by 7 a.m. I had brought a book along to help pass the time, but I reread the same page ten times without remembering anything. Actually I kept scanning Stanley Pool* from one end of Mbamou Island to the other, hoping to catch a glimpse of the boat. At 8.30 I entered the office and asked the white man there if such a delay was expected.

'What boat are you waiting for?'

'The *Fondère*.'

'But the *Fondère* arrived last night, my dear man. And not even at this dock.'

He took me outside and pointed to a boat moored in the distance.

I immediately headed for Apolline's apartment. I told myself she must have arrived late at night and preferred not to awaken me. She would still be in bed.

It takes about one hour to walk from the harbour to Louémé Street. Brazzaville is laid out lengthwise, designed only for those privileged few who can afford a car. I hailed a

*The lake-like expansion of the Congo River near Brazzaville.

taxi. My heart was beating hard as we approached the house. I knocked. No one answered. I walked around the building but only found an old woman, Apolline's landlady, grinding her *saca-saca*.

'Isn't Apolline here, Mother?'

'Yes.'

'She's here?'

'No, son. She's gone out.'

'Did she say where she was going?'

She must be at my place. I ran to reach home before she left. The news there was no better.

'Samba, has anyone come to see me?'

'No.'

'Are you sure?'

'I already told you. No one came.'

'Not even when you were asleep?'

'Hey, come on! Who do you think I am, Rockefeller, to be able to sleep until 8 o'clock. And with all the noise you made this morning …'

I went to the university and searched among the students of English but did not find her. I had no idea where else to go or what to do. We feel well protected behind our habits, our ideas. But one unexpected occurrence is enough to upset our plans, to make a man feel alone, fallen from a caravan crossing the desert, unsure of what to cling to and in which direction to go. I was certain Apolline was in Brazzaville but couldn't find her. I decided it would be better to return home. Sooner or later she would come looking for me. When I got home, Samba had left. I asked my neighbours if anyone had knocked on the door. Of course no one could really give me a precise answer which only irritated me. As I opened the door, I hoped to find a note slipped underneath as Apolline had often done in the past. Again I was disappointed. I tried to reason with myself. I had so often stated I could take anything, even the destruction of the world as long as I had something to read. Was it possible that such a small thing as a cancelled date could so upset me? The books I tried to read seemed insipid. I

25

found some of Jonas' cigarettes and smoked almost the whole pack. Four times I went to Apolline's apartment, but in vain. And I wasted the whole day.

As I was getting ready to go to the university restaurant for dinner, she came. In my great joy to see her, I didn't even think of being angry. She was there, and I asked for nothing more. As soon as we were in my room, we threw ourselves into each other's arms, and I lost no time in turning out the light.

I thought Apolline got up from the bed unusually quickly. Generally she was the one to hold me back, saying:

'You men, once you're satisfied, you turn your backs on us and think only of a cigarette.'

This time I found myself playing the role of the woman. Apolline seemed to have lost her usual tenderness.

'Is anything wrong?'

'No.'

'Yes there is. You seem angry with me.'

'As usual you're making yourself miserable by trying to analyze everything too much.'

I thought life would continue much as it had before vacation. But Apolline reminded me we had to work harder. Only four months were left before exams. She was right. I reprimanded myself for having sunk so low as to need a reminder from her. I thought I had disappointed her. She had given herself to me because she admired me, and because I was the only fellow she could respect intellectually and academically. And I had shown myself spineless and commonplace when in love. I resolved to shake myself out of it, all the while harbouring a certain resentment at hearing her warnings against the delights towards which she, like a spoilt child, had led me.

'We must behave now. We can only meet twice a week.'

That was a real shock. But I was used to keeping to a strict schedule, abiding by rules. I drew a certain satisfaction from seeing how far I could push myself. So we agreed to go out Wednesdays and Saturdays. But for two whole weeks I stayed at home. She was obliged to accept an invitation from a cousin she had not seen often, and go out with a girl friend from Point-Noir who was passing through. She had been bored and thought about me the whole time, but on Saturday she needed the time to catch up on her studies.

Didn't Apolline realize that this was a greater punishment for me than the penitences we had sometimes been called upon to perform at the seminary? Formerly, I had been particularly fond of Saturday evenings because I was assured of the uninterrupted solitude I needed for my vice – reading. Saturday was the one day of the week when everyone was so preoccupied with going out dancing that no one thought about disturbing me. I could read until late at night without having to get up early on Sunday. But since I had met Apolline, Saturday night had become our favourite night together. Now, accustomed to partaking of this elixir, I found it difficult to return to my strict diet. My feeling of frustration awakened a resentment toward her, the person who had formerly been the dearest in the world to me. Sometimes this feeling was obvious in my behaviour.

'You've been especially warm and loving to me lately,' she told me.

And immediately I reproached myself for my insensitivity.

When we went to the cinema or for a walk – which, I repeat, became less and less frequent – I noticed she tried to prevent me from holding her hand.

One evening we were planning to go out after I had begged her several times. I waited in my room, as if prepared to spend the whole night at my desk.

'Aren't you ready yet? And women are always blamed for being the late ones!'

I don't remember exactly what I answered, but my tone was quite cold. She was hurt and I almost begged for forgiveness. But I had decided once and for all to clarify the situation. It was our first argument. She cried. I too was confused because I don't like to see people suffer, to see people cry. And when I am the cause, it becomes unbearable.

27

'It's not my fault,' she hiccupped between sobs.

When she was in a condition to talk, it was her turn to break my heart.

Her vacation had been awful, hardly a vacation at all. Starting the day after her arrival home, she had faced repeated and successive verbal attacks by her father, mother and family council. They knew she was 'living with' a Lari. People of that tribe are strong-headed and untrustworthy. Yet she had rejected the diamond merchant although he too came from Mossaka. Had she forgotten that her father owed his position to him? In fact, Apolline's father ran a shop owned by her former fiancé. Recently her father had been threatened by the man who wanted to reclaim the business which had been the dowry given in exchange for the girl. How would her father pay for the schooling of her five sisters?

'If it were only up to me, I wouldn't give in. I reject those old prejudices. But I don't feel I have the fight to reduce my parents to paupers or compromise the future of my sisters. And one never knows, with their magic charms ...'

'Go on, Apolline, continue. Justify it however you want. I'm not listening anymore. You must know that by talking like this you're killing me. I too, would have to explain to my tribe. I too would have been faced with a pressure to abandon you. I never said anything about it, just as I didn't speak of the pain I felt simply from the thought that a hypocritically devout person would point me out because I took up with a girl so soon after leaving the seminary. My love for you also implied struggles against my social class and its prejudices. I accepted all that thinking – ours would be a joint fight and there was no need to speak of it. And I thought you were the more mature, the stronger one. How can I tie myself to a weaker person when the world is full of difficult battles to be fought?'

Even her allusion to the magic charms did not make me laugh. We walked toward the river and climbed to the top floor of a hotel which overlooked Stanley Pool. We followed the slow rhythm of the many green islands which looked like a funeral procession, marching towards the Djoué. A young couple was seated having drinks. They were full of tenderness for each other that evening. Their eyes, their demeanour spoke of their love. Our romanticism was of a resigned, gloomy, unhappy nature. But still I wonder if we weren't at our most tender with each other that evening. We had lived a great passion. Society condemned it in the name of wisdom. We would have to resign ourselves. What good were melodramatic scenes? We were too intellectual and possessed too much good taste. We would help each other have the strength to be from then on no more than good friends. Or so we believed at that moment.

I avoided going to class for fear of meeting her. She didn't miss a single one. I worked at home, but my room was filled with her presence. I couldn't stay there for more than an hour. I decided to work in the library. Several times I met her and it was very difficult for me. Even when chance didn't throw us together, I still found it hard to work. I saw Apolline in the eyes of my friends. Although they didn't dare say anything, I divined their thoughts. He who paraded around so with the beautiful Apolline now finds himself alone today. Ha, ha, ha! I heard their silent laughter. That was when I began to spend more time with Kodia.

Kodia had been a teacher and, by working diligently by himself, managed to pass a special exam allowing him entrance to the university. Now, on leave from his teaching duties, he was working on a degree in physics. He was both older and more mature than the rest of us, a sort of young surrogate father whom we respected but who understood our problems in a way that our real fathers, men of a different generation and a different age, were unable to do. Kodia was a dedicated activist. He led the student movement with an infectious enthusiasm. While the other militants – those I called the 'fanatics' – argued for or against imperialism, Kodia questioned me about my studies. Philosophy interested him and he asked many questions about philosophers whom, I thought, couldn't possibly hold much interest for a Marxist–Leninist like himself. Philosophers like Husserl and

29

Kierkegaard. Beginning with subjects as apparently apolitical as liberty or death he managed, without shocking me, to demonstrate the necessity of an anti-imperialist struggle which no longer seemed just a slogan but a fundamental, vital philosophy. When I think about it today, I see him as a sort of Father Flandrin.

One day I opened up my heart to Kodia and told him of my relationship with Apolline. I confessed how it had destroyed me inside. He listened in silence. When I had finished, he looked at me fixedly, took out a cigarette which he lit with the butt of the one he was finishing, and told me about his marriage. The woman he lived with was unconcerned about the problems he was consumed by – the problems related to the future of Africa – and it was a great sorrow for him.

'Yet I married her against the will of my family.'

'But the interests you miss having in common with your wife are exactly what Apolline and I shared. And I know that in the whole Congo there isn't another girl like her.'

He looked at me, smiled and inhaled deeply.

'You may be right. But what good does it do to dwell on it? Once a plate is broken you might as well throw it away. Of course it can be mended, but it will never again be the same plate, will no longer be the beloved object. All your thoughts are parasitic. It's like a man who has lost an arm. He can continue to compare himself to others, and lament his lost arm and the time he had two good ones. That reaction would be perfectly normal, and only a beast would make fun of him. But this one-armed man would be an unhappy person, bitter, disagreeable to himself and to others. On the other hand, if he tried to overcome his infirmity, he would glow with an inner contentment. He would be happy. Your problem is the same. I understand your pain. It shows that your heart is sensitive and rich. But if you don't rise above it, you'll be lost.'

'It's not easy to reason with oneself concerning love.'

'Yes, that's true. One doesn't forget so easily. And if you

30

continue to live alone, you won't be able to forget.'

The daily conversation slowly affected me. I threw myself into the student movement. I even abandoned my studies. I had a strong wish to stand out, to be the leader who would be spoken of on the radio. That would be my revenge. Each time Apolline would turn on her radio and hear my name, I would disturb her tranquillity. She would miss me.

One day the movement sent me to the Sangha region to give a series of talks on alienation. I rediscovered my own native country. It was perhaps the only week when I didn't think about her.

When I returned, I found a white envelope on my table. Inside was a folded card announcing the marriage of Apolline to her diamond merchant.

***

The snow has been falling all day. I haven't even set foot outside. For two years now I have been studying in the USSR, far from the arena which devastated my adolescent heart. The work is all-absorbing and the day's routine makes us forget our small problems. I have known women here, some more beautiful and enriching than Apolline. But I always have the impression with them that I am acting the way you were with me Apolline, in our best moments. My passion for study returned long ago. I share the ideals of those who dream of a world without loneliness. Nonetheless, on days like today when it snows, I think of you, Apolline, you who have never seen this perfect white which blankets the sleeping world. And I feel alone.

THE ESTEEMED
REPRESENTATIVE

'… Colonization has imposed an economic system on us that has reduced our sisters to slaves. At the present stage, it's up to the men to liberate the underprivileged of our society in general, and our women in particular, from this economic servitude.' (Applause.) 'Our women have a right to certain jobs and they must be allowed to hold them. It is unacceptable in an independent country like ours, where thousands of girls are educated, that only the foreigners in our country get jobs as secretaries and saleswomen.' (Applause.) 'Sisters, let us take advantage of the occasion of your conference to publicly ask our National Assembly and our government, "Why the delay?" What is holding up the passage of a law explicitly spelling out that all positions as waitresses in bars and night clubs are to be exclusively reserved for Africans, and prohibited to Europeans.' (Everyone in the hall rose, and thundering applause drowned out the speaker.) 'The salaries earned by our women in these jobs must be equal to those earned by European women.' (Thunderous applause.) 'Because as was said by – um – um– as was said by – uh – La Fontaine, I believe it was La Fontaine … (Applause.) … As I said, La Fontaine stated, "Equal pay for equal work". (Thundering applause.) It is also time that those fathers, who in the name of tradition still refuse to allow their daughters to continue their schooling, be disillusioned of their prejudices. Women have the same rights as men. Yet some men still refuse to accept this truth. That is why I am turning to you, my sisters, and proclaiming that you women alone must liberate yourselves from masculine tyranny.' (Applause.) 'At the present time, when tribal divisions are strong and men throughout the world are mercilessly killing each other like lunatics, let me say in front of you, up here on this platform, that only women can help us to overcome tribal prejudices and win peace on earth.' (Applause.)

Representative Ngouakou-Ngouakou continued to speak in this manner for twenty minutes, watch in hand. When he had finished, he wiped his brow. The crowd in the lecture room at the party headquarters broke out in a frenzied joy. Men and women congratulated each other with slaps on the back, laughed and shouted out, 'Papa Ngouakou-Ngouakou! Is it Papa Ngouakou-Ngouakou?' 'Yes, yes.' responded another part of the room. Some of the women danced in place while the babies they carried on their backs grimaced at being so rudely awakened from their naps.

The bodyguard ceremoniously removed the official shoulder sash from the speaker and carried off the folder in which was sandwiched the text of the speech Ngouakou-Ngouakou had just delivered. The excited crowd, given over to rejoicing, could not calm down.

**

At 8 p.m. Ngouakou-Ngouakou returned home. His houseboy hurried to relieve him of his briefcase. He threw himself into an arm chair.

'Bouka, Bouka, come say hello to Papa.'

The child climbed into his father's lap. Ngouakou-Ngouakou surveyed him proudly, his only son, his seventh child.

'Papa, you didn't buy me an Apollo XII.'

'What in the world is that?'

'Akpa has one. His father bought it for him.'

'Emilienne,' shouted Ngouakou-Ngouakou. 'Emilienne!'

'She is writing a paper for school,' called her mother from the kitchen.

'Writing? A paper? Writing won't teach her how to please her husband. Tell her to bring me my slippers.'

'Listen, Ngouakou-Ngouakou. Be a little more understanding of that poor child,' said her mother.

'Tell me, woman, since when do wives talk back to their husbands? Are you going to teach me how to bring up my daughter?'

'Here, Papa, here are your slippers,' said Bouka-Bouka.

'Thank you, son. At least you think of me. But this is really too much. Are we men going to have to do the work around here now?'

'Emilienne!'

Emilienne arrived, all distraught.

'Well now, how many times must I call you?'

'I'm sorry, Papa. I didn't hear you.'

'Where were you?'

'In my room.'

'In your room? You must have been dreaming.'

'No, Papa, I was doing my maths homework.'

'Dreaming and mathematics don't go together. If you were studying maths, you should have been paying attention. And when one pays attention, one hears people call. Bring me some whiskey.'

Emilienne mechanically headed towards the cupboard. She was dreaming of boarding school, and envying her friends who were far from familial discipline. It must be nice to depend only on oneself. Parents! They think they're acting for our benefit with all their rules. They don't even see that we're judging them. Oh! The bottle is almost empty. Emilienne searched in vain on all the shelves of the cupboard.

'How about my whiskey?'

'There isn't any more.'

'What? There isn't any more? I forbid you to play with your friends for two days.'

'But Papa, it's not my fault.'

'You have to learn that when the bottle is only half full, it's time to go and buy another one. Bring me a beer, then.'

He turned on the TV. Myriam Makeba was singing. Usually he enjoyed listening to her, but that evening she got on his nerves. They were showing the tape of her most recent concert in the city. Ngouakou-Ngouakou knew it by heart, since it was broadcast at least twice a week. When the TV producers run out of ideas for shows, they fall back on something they have on hand, even if the public has already seen it a hundred times. Ngouakou-Ngouakou was bored. He checked his watch.

'When can we eat?'

'In five minutes,' answered his wife from the kitchen.

'I'm hungry.'

'The rice isn't quite ready yet.'

'It's always the same story. Nothing is ever ready at the right time.'

Myriam Makeba was singing 'Malaïka'. Ngouakou-Ngouakou let himself be carried away by the music this time. He liked beautiful songs. Then the South African singer chose one in which she clicked her tongue and danced, swaying her backside about like a boat on the waves.

'Dinner is ready,' called his wife.

Ngouakou-Ngouakou did not answer.

'Dinner! It's getting cold.'

Ngouakou-Ngouakou curbed his anger. He disliked being interrupted when he was listening to music. He sat down at his place, facing the TV. Myriam continued to sing.

'Rice and meat with sauce again?'

'At this time of year there isn't much choice at the market.'

'Not much choice? Isn't there any fish?'

'That must be the first time I ever heard you offer any suggestions about meals. It's a fine idea to vary the menu, but there are limits. In the morning when I ask you what you want for dinner, you grab your briefcase and dash off to the office.'

'That's the last straw! Don't you think I have enough to handle without having to think about meals on top of it all? You don't go off to work in an office. I'm the one who brings in the money.'

'I would gladly change places.'

'What I do isn't woman's work. I know many women who dream of being in your place, of having a husband who provides the latest model gas stove, a refrigerator, money ...'

'Money? With the money you give me every week I have to rack my brain to feed a large family like ours.'

'Obviously you're not the one earning the money!'
The newscaster began presenting the national news.

'Shut up all of you so I can hear!'

> 'Today marked the opening of the conference sponsored by the National Federation of Radical Women. Several speakers were on the day's roster. This is the second conference of the Federation since its inception. Those present included delegations invited from neighbouring African countries and from friendly countries in Europe, America and Asia.'

Ngouakou-Ngouakou was furious. Tomorrow I'll speak with the Minister of Information about punishing the newscaster. He didn't even mention my speech. Ngouakou-Ngouakou pushed away his plate.

'I'm not hungry anymore.'

The newscaster spoke about the war in Nigeria. Ngouakou-Ngouakou lit a cigarette, thinking how they always seemed to repeat the same things about the war.

'How about the girls? Can't they help you with the cooking and housework? Marcelline, how about you?'

'But Papa, I have a lot of work.'

'Don't forget you're a woman. A woman's most important work is to keep house.'

'Be a little more understanding,' cautioned her mother. 'You know perfectly well that Marcelline is in her last year at school and is preparing for her exams so she can receive her diploma.'

'Do you think a diploma will help her keep her husband at home? Good food will help, yes, and something else too.'

'You could at least be more discrete in what you say.'

36

'Oh Papa,' cried Bouka-Bouka, 'Look!'

Featured on the television were young Biafran children. They looked like fat-bellied skeletons. The whole family fell silent.

'Why are those children so ugly?'

'It's not their fault,' corrected his mother.

Ngouakou-Ngouakou stood up and went to his room. Whistling, he threw his clothes on to the bed. His wife would tidy up after him. He pulled on a pair of light grey trousers, and a short, loose-fitting, bright-coloured shirt decorated with gold braiding on the sleeves, pockets and collar. He looked at himself in the mirror. He looked younger. He lit a cigarette and went out into the night, whistling.

***

The Peek-a-Boo bar is located on the outskirts of the city, on an unlit street. The bar itself, though, has electricity. This came about because the owner, Marguerita, is a remarkably beautiful young widow with regular features, well-formed breasts peeping out from behind her camisole, and long fawn-like legs that are difficult to ignore when she wears her tight-fitting dresses and high-heeled shoes. Some mistake her for a mulatto, but those who have known her since birth say that her skin tint has lightened considerably since certain American products have been for sale in the Congo. Marguerita is very popular. And since she is unable to satisfy everyone at once, she has cousins living with her, cousins almost as beautiful as she is. Whenever a high-level official brings a group of visiting dignitaries to the Peek-a-Boo Bar, he flaunts his prowess by arranging for them to dance cheek to cheek with Marguerita. At about one in the morning he whispers in her ear and goes off to 'make it' with her while her cousins 'make it' with the foreign dignitaries. In exchange for these favours, Marguerita obtains what she wants. Two months of constant attention to the Minister of Energy resulted in the installation of electricity in her bar.

Marie-Therese had taken a taxi to reach that part of the city. She hesitated a moment before entering the bar. The electricity, used mostly to power the record player, hardly lit the room. The light bulbs were all painted red so that only red shadows were distinguishable moving about or seated at the bar. The room was divided into small compartments, separated by bamboo partitions. People seated in these compartments were protected from unwelcome glances. Marie-Therese chose one and sat down on a small, low, willow bench. Marguerita had seen her and signalled to one of her cousins who went over to the new customer, shuffling her feet.

'No thank you, nothing for the moment. I'm waiting for someone.'

When the cousin returned to the bar, a man who had been seated on a high stool grabbed her around the waist and led her off to dance the rumba. The cousin immediately lost her indifference. The two, pelvis to pelvis, moved with large, circular rubbing movements. They have nothing left to hide from each other, thought Marie-Therese. If the lights weren't so dim we would surely see that their eyes are closed. Marie-Therese felt embarrassed by the display.

When the dance ended, the man returned to the bar and flirted laughingly with all the cousins. As the next dance began, he approached Marie-Therese. His self-assurance and beautiful eyes seemed to paralyse her.

'No thank you.'

'Do you find me so unattractive?'

'…'

She turned her head away and just at that moment Ngouakou-Ngouakou entered.

'Oh, excuse me, Representative, Sir. Excuse me … I didn't know …'

Ngouakou-Ngouakou said nothing. He turned away, sat down and mumbled to himself: 'It's that little idiot Bwala. He'll find out who he's talking to.'

The cousin returned. She joked informally with the esteemed representative for a few minutes. They knew each other well. The Honourable Representative Ngouakou-Ngouakou is one of the humblest men in the world. He is a child of the proletariat and has no fear of renewing his relations with the masses. He ordered drinks. When the waitress returned with the order and the politician started to pay, she told him that it had already been taken care of by the man at the bar.

A *pachanga* was playing and Marie-Therese wanted to dance. Since no one else was on the floor, everyone at the bar watched as she danced with Ngouakou-Ngouakou, and they smiled. They smiled to see a young girl show off her youth through every movement of her hips, legs and shoulders as she moved to the music, smiling wholesomely. Were they also smiling tenderly at the fifty-year old man whose baldness and paunch did not inhibit his nimble movement? The man at the bar could not resist remarking:

'Yes, sister, that's Africa for you! Our negritude, our blackness. Our's is the civilization of the dance.'

But the dancing couple took no notice of their audience at the bar. They were too engrossed in each other.

After three dances, Ngouakou-Ngouakou wanted to leave.

'Already!' she asked. 'But it's so nice here.'

'It'll be nicer somewhere else.' He took her by the arm, helped her up, and disappeared with her into the dark night.

***

In front of the Hotel Relais, Ngouakou-Ngouakou repeated to Marie-Therese:

'I had my secretary reserve a room in the name of Miss Baker. Go to the reception desk, and ask for the key. Wait for me in the room. I'll join you there in fifteen minutes.'

As she turned out the light, Marie-Therese felt herself engulfed by strong, well-muscled arms. The hair on her arms intermingled with her partner's. He was panting already. It was always like that with him. He didn't caress her, but preferred to enter her immediately. She could not help crying out, from the depths of her throat, as if in pain.

39

'Am I hurting you?'

'No, just the opposite.'

Her nails dug into his flesh. She felt his large muzzle move across her face. She could no longer speak, but only pant, 'yes, yes,' and other things she could not make out herself. It always took him a long time, longer than the young men. She liked that. She knew she was damned. But so what. She vibrated, she lived, she was free.

Four times that night she whimpered and cried out, before finally falling asleep. Each time she repeated:

'Oh, it feels so good! You're pitiless to satisfy me like that.'

She dreamed that Ngouakou-Ngouakou came to pick her up in a large, fancy American car. Dressed in black, she was elated. He told her that his wife was dead. He had come directly from the funeral to fetch her and take her abroad. She hardly dared believe it. She wanted to pack some *pagnes** and dresses to take along but Ngouakou-Ngouakou warned her not to waste time.

After helping her into the car, Ngouakou-Ngouakou sped to the airport. Along the way she saw many familiar faces in the street. Despite the speed of the car, she distinctly heard them condemning her for taking an old man away from his children and accusing her of having killed Mrs Ngouakou-Ngouakou. Marie-Therese was dripping with sweat by the time they reached the airport. There was no room on the plane so they were put in the cockpit. Ngouakou-Ngouakou took command of the controls and started the engines. The plane moved along the runway but did not manage to get more than ten feet off the ground. It seemed as if the black dog which had been following Marie-Therese would manage to jump into the plane.

Marie-Therese woke up and saw Ngouakou-Ngouakou already dressed.

'I must leave now.'

She reached out to him and smiled. He sat on the edge of the bed, kissed her on the forehead and said: 'I have to go.'

*Cloth worn wrapped about the body. The traditional dress of African women.

'But I have something to tell you.'

'You're just looking for a way to keep me here with you.'

'No, it's important.'

She took the man's hand and placed it on her belly under the sheet.

I think I'm carrying your child.

'What? You're joking!'

'No, it's true.'

'What proof do you have that it's mine?'

Marie-Therese turned on her stomach, buried her head in the pillow, bit and bit it, and started to cry. She beat the bed with her fists and kicked her feet.

'What's wrong, honey?'

'Bastard, you bastard! Get out of here. Bastard, bastard, bastard ...'

***

The sun poked its head over the horizon, and climbed slowly in the sky, promising a hot day. Shining through the windows, the daylight awakened Miss Ngouakou-Ngouakou. As was her custom every morning, she turned on the radio to keep herself from falling back to sleep. She listened to the national news.

> 'Yesterday Representative Ngouakou-Ngouakou presented a keynote address at the opening session of the Radical Women's Federation Conference. In his speech he stressed the need to liberate our women, who are not inferior beings but are men's equals.'

THE VETERAN

It was not long after the *coup d'état* that I realized the young officers were cheating on us. True, they were the ones who had urged us to participate in the conspiracy against President Takana*, and we hadn't thought twice about risking our necks in preparing the coup. In point of fact, I had been easy to convince. I hadn't asked for a penny. The atmosphere, after three years of Takana's regime, was unbearable. Although officially the government included representatives from all the regions and ethnic groups of the country, in reality an inner circle from his tribe, including the Minister of the Interior, were the ones who actually wielded the power, advising the president on his daily decisions. Since my tribe has always ruled over Takana's, I saw my participation in the rebellion as a duty. The militia that fought against those idiots who objected to paying taxes and performing the menial tasks ordered by the French commanders was, from the time of the white man's arrival, always conscripted from my region of the country. And I am the son and the grandson of a chief. From childhood on, the members of my family were taught to be leaders. Whereas this Takana – may he rot in prison where we've thrown him – is the son of a slave. He was brought up by a family I know and was allowed by them to learn to read and write. His lower class mentality is what drove him to play for such large stakes and contributed to his downfall.

*Fictitious character.

42

Each pleasure was new to him. For example, he absolutely adored women. Single or married, he wanted them all to parade through his bed. He considered it his exclusive right to deflower all the young, stunning and most desirable female citizens. Once at a cocktail party he was literally bewitched by a young, beautiful stranger. She was wearing a long, white, flowing Senegalese *boubou* that evening, and seemed to have been moulded by the hands of the most skilled craftsman. He asked for an introduction. She was the wife of a young lieutenant who had just returned home. Takana did everything he could, used all the influence of his position, to convince her to accept his attentions. Nothing swayed her. In anger, he arranged for her husband to be transferred to the bush, 800 miles from the capital. Finally he discovered a plot in which the lieutenant could be implicated. He summoned the woman and renewed his requests, offering in exchange the freedom of her husband. It is said she slapped him in the face. In his rage, he threatened to execute the man, but did not have time to carry out his order. Our coup happened to succeed in time.

At first I was named Minister of Defence. You should have seen how I was applauded. I must admit I greatly enjoyed participating in parades, surrounded by an escort on motorcycles. None of the young men in the Revolutionary Liberation Council or in the government possessed my natural physical presence. You can immediately see by the carriage of a man if he is destined to lead. Small talk, both at Council meetings or in the government quickly bored me. Our country doesn't need frivolity, but rather a strong, energetic man. Yes, a man like me, who knows how to give orders and who, flanked by the army, would put everyone to work. Our country needs to be militarized because, as the white men say, we care too much for talk and not enough for work.

I had already planned out my entire strategy. From Chad I would bring in former Sara sharpshooters as technical assistants to our army. They would oversee the work of all the niggers. I would install loud speakers in each town, in each street, to broadcast my orders. Everyone who refused to obey would be punished by the Sara militia. Second offenders would simply be done away with. In this way everyone would march in step with my rhythm: one, two, one, two … In a few years we would surge ahead.

But as I already said, those youngsters cheated on me. While I was preparing to leave on a diplomatic mission to France and a meeting with the General to request his support, (I would have been made a general and, between equals, we would have understood each other completely) they reshuffled the government and sent me as ambassador here, to Algeria, a country where I had fought on the side of the French and won honours in the French army.

What a bitter pill to swallow! For four years I had fought against the *fellahin*, the Algerian nationals, just as I had previously fought in Morocco and Tunisia. There, in fact, is where I earned my stripes. Here, in official speeches and in private conversation, all everyone talks about are the days of resistance against the French, of the *maquis* resistance fighters, and so on and so forth.

I finally began adjusting to my situation. One day I confided in the French ambassador. He understood my feelings perfectly and explained how we should leave the past behind. Wasn't it even harder for him? He introduced me into new circles, to French people and diplomats, so that finally I came to prefer life here to life in our provincial capital.

And oh, how I love the city of Algiers. It's a true metropolis, with tall houses and wide streets, full of carts and people. I'm partial to large modern cities, bustling with life, where one is just another face in the crowd. Dakar, Abidjan, Kinshasa – those are real capital cities. You know, if I were in power (maybe it will still come one day) I would ask the Americans to beautify our capital too. I would entice rich white men from around the world to open large stores like those in Paris.

And – oh yes – Algiers has its share of beautiful women. Let me tell you! That's important! Before my wife arrived I met

44

one. Wow! You should see her. Her name is Nadia. She reminds me of some of the mulatto women at home, with her golden, willow-coloured, varnished skin. But our mulattos don't have such straight, soft hair. And her eyes are so black she needs no make-up. Her way of looking at people is what first caught my eye.

For six months now I have been seeing her. Last Saturday I promised to take her dancing at Tipaza. She méntioned that a Congolese orchestra was booked there for the season. You know how those people are masters of the art. How could I refuse? And when she looks at me, I can't deny her anything. I concocted a story about a formal bachelors' dinner in order to leave my wife at home.

We danced until two in the morning. Then we went to a hotel where I had reserved a room. At about three o'clock I said to her:

'Hey my little dove, are you asleep?'

'Dove! Why do you call me that?'

'For no special reason.'

She put her head back down on my shoulder. But I could feel her tension. Then something wet touched my chest. At first I thought it was the sweat dripping from our touching bodies. But soon it was undeniable: she was crying.

'What's the matter?'

No answer. She couldn't possibly be angry with me. Never before had I been as gentle with a woman as with Nadia. She had been so happy a moment earlier.

Did her tears mean she knew our love was a dead end, despite the special chemistry between us? It was unfair to ask her if that were the problem. I began kissing her all over, caressing her straight, soft, silky hair in which my fingers always found such pleasure. Finally she broke away and sat up on the edge of the bed.

'No, it's nothing. It's not your fault. Only – my mother used to call me her little dove.'

'Did you love your mother?'

'Yes, of course.'

'She's no longer alive?'

Nadia told me the circumstances of her mother's death. She herself had attended school in Oran. Her father led an arm of the National Liberation Front in her native region of Saïda. His *nom-de-guerre* had been Lightning Moustapha. Shortly before independence, the French secured precise information on him. One day they picked up her mother for questioning. They took her to prison and tried to pressure her into denouncing her husband or someone else in the movement.

'She was a remarkable woman endowed with exceptional courage. She wouldn't betray my father. I only learned of her arrest on Saturday when I came home for the weekend. When I returned to school I was crushed. I couldn't work in that place full of French girls, supporters of the same people who, at the very moment, were torturing my mother. But yet I was proud of being the daughter of a heroine. After one month they released her. They didn't press charges against her. But she had changed. Previously so beautiful and fresh, she had become white-haired and wrinkled. After her release from prison, I didn't return to school again. My mother arranged to have me evacuated to Morocco and went herself into the mountains. Not as a nurse but as a combatant. She died with a gun in her hand, in a fight against the French imperialist army.'

'In the Saïda region?' I asked.

'Yes.'

'In what year?'

'1960.' And she told me the month.

I got up and dressed. Nadia is one of the few people in Algeria who don't know I had seen combat in the country. But I, too, can't forget that fight against the *fellahin* in 1960. They fought well and were all killed. And yes, there had been a woman among the dead.

Nadia, I will never see you again. I can no longer carry on anything but the most superficial conversation with people in this country, because I always fear stumbling on a relative or close friend of someone I killed or ordered killed.

Oh, how I long to be relieved of my post.

THE HONOURABLE GENTLEMAN

Perhaps I should have kept quiet, filed away my report, let the leaders handle the affair. Because the more I think about it, the more I feel I'm fighting a losing battle. The outcome would have been the same had I protested, reasoned, threatened, or held my peace. Now the case is most certainly closed.

One morning the Director called me into his office.

'Dahounka, I have an important job for you. I'm sending you to Maxiville immediately to investigate the employment practices there and assess the prospects for the next ten years. Get a look at the relevant documents. If you merely speak to the European managers, they'll throw sand in your eyes. They don't have any interest in our arranging to replace them. I'm sending you there to unearth the facts.'

I was pleased with my assignment. Maxiville is 200 miles from the capital and I had never been there. It's a town that sprang up out of the bush when copper was discovered. In a region where previously there had been no inhabitants, IMA (Incorporated Mining Association) constructed a compound which stands in sharp contrast to its surroundings. Upon emerging from the dense bush one comes smack upon the town, well-laid out and landscaped, with neat paths, complete with carefully tended lawns, and containing twenty or so houses placed in a pleasant, carefully designed random-looking arrangement each one as attractive and comfortable as the next. The modern, sophisticated world amidst the wild, primitive one. Everything was thought of: a cinema, club, swimming pool with water as green as dioptase and clear as glass right there in the middle of a bilharzia-infested region.

There is even a restaurant and two cottages for guests of the company or people wishing to take advantage of the remoteness of the place. My accommodation was better than what I am used to at home. The house assigned to me, small yet comfortable and elegant, was at once well conceived and simple. In fact the engineer who toured me around the property stressed that aspect too much for my taste, as if to emphasize that everything can be created from nothing, a fact still not grasped by the Africans.

I was also shown all the social services provided by the company. 'Because, after all, we're working for the good of the country (which, of course, we love).'

An area of cabins, sporting conical roofs, had been built for the miners which those d... ......(here he restrained his language) quickly ruined. So now they and their wives are being offered free courses in reading and writing which also serves as a means to teach them rules of social behaviour. And take my word for it, the country will reap the benefits in the end without being called on to pay a cent. Attractive classrooms had been built for the workers' children. The teachers were housed by the company, books and materials supplied gratis. I don't remember having seen anywhere in the country a cleaner, better-equipped hospital than the infirmary at Maxiville. Systematically, every two weeks, a team of miners is thoroughly examined. A little like astronauts. I was told that they were even fed especially rich food. The work there is so difficult they have to be overnourished.

But all this is only possible because of the copper mines. The company claims to earn twenty-eight billion CFA francs a year, twice our entire national budget. Since the Government is a stockholder, it receives four billion.

In the evening I ate dinner at the company restaurant. All the single, white-collar workers eat there. Upon entering, I felt as though I were on an ocean liner. Neon lights, waiters in white jackets and black trousers, the bar stocked with every choice of drink that an up-to-date night club might offer and tables covered with white cloths and set with heavy silverware all made it easy to forget that around us people slept on straw mats on the ground, in huts lit only with old hurricane lamps. My guide of the afternoon invited me to join him at his table. He introduced me to two other professionals who were dining with him.

At the beginning we had little to say to each other.

'May I offer you some soup?'

'No, thank you.'

'You really should try some. It's one of the specialities of the house.'

'Could you please pass the bread?'

'Thank you.'

'You're welcome.'

'Would you like some wine?'

I believe I was the one to finally break the ice although I don't really remember how it started. There was a moment when we were recalling our school years, and as the conversation progressed, I discovered that one of the men had known some of my colleagues from advanced maths class. The conversation warmed up and my companions even became friendly.

'You should have mentioned earlier that you'd studied in France.' A veritable verbal battle ensued as to who would buy me a brandy. They begged me to accompany them to the camp cinema. I would have preferred to retire early. The trip by Land Rover had been draining and, before falling asleep, I wanted to take advantage of being alone to read a novel I had brought along, which my hectic life in town prevented me from reading.

'You don't have anything better to do. Come along.'

How could I explain to the young engineers, who had come to this back-woods town only to earn enough to move up the social ladder at home, that I found reading Chinua Achebe much more intoxicating than a talk with friends, an evening

49

spent dancing, or a bad American film. Our conversation had been enough to convince me that although they were nice enough fellows, undoubtedly loyal friends, undeniably competent in their work, they were unexpectedly dull when discussing anything besides chemistry or physics.

I don't remember either the name of the film or the plot. I simply know that the engineers laughed their heads off. It helped them 'unwind' they told me afterwards. They didn't even notice my discomfort when a nigger appeared on the screen and opened his eyes wide as saucers because he saw move what he had mistaken for a mannequin. He was made to cry out in terror and swear that it was a work of the devil until a white man pointed out his error and calmed him down.

'Good night. Wasn't it a good film?'

The following morning my work really began. I had to wait more than an hour in the anteroom before being received by the general manager. When I explained the reason for my visit, he told me that what I wanted was impossible.

'But I was sent here by order of the Cabinet Minister. And the Regional Governor himself expressed no objections when contacted on the matter.'

'According to the terms of the contract we signed with your government, it is impossible.'

'My dear sir, let me repeat that I am here by order of the Cabinet Minister.'

'What importance do you think the Minister's orders have for me compared to the contract? Ministers come and go, my friend, but the contract remains. And it guarantees the privacy of the documents you have requested.'

This was said gently, with a smile, even a certain charm and friendliness, so that normally the conversation should have continued. But it so happens that for me content counts more than form.

'You've said something very serious.'

I don't know how I managed to make my way out of his office.

***

50

'You say that Mr Vuillaume actually pronounced those very words?'

'Yes, Governor.'

'Now make absolutely sure of what you say. Could you please repeat his exact words? Take it down carefully, Mrs Ngouoka. Yes, it's a very serious business. Those Europeans think they can do anything they wish. They forget we are now independent.'

The Governor immediately had Mr Vuillaume, manager of IMA, summoned to his office.

I had known the Governor when we were both boarders at secondary school. Ndoté was older. When I was in my second year he was about to graduate, but unlike his classmates, he did not look down on us greenhorns. He always smiled. I even wished to be like him and hoped to maintain the sort of contact he had with the younger students when I was in my last year. At soccer games, Ndoté kept his temper whether he won or lost. If he threw his opponent off balance during a scuffle, he would go over to him when the play was finished, excuse himself, and make sure the boy had not been hurt. He always participated in strikes against the principal without having to be recruited, but never cried out 'Gaston is a thief' or 'Gaston is an imperialist pig' because it was totally foreign to his nature to insult anyone, even someone who had done him wrong. Ndoté was a brilliant student. I heard that each year from sixth grade on, he had won a prize for excellence. Yet he always listened attentively and patiently even to the sort of nonsense which idiots like Faliko or little Samba spewed forth. Ndoté was what one calls a good friend.

I met him again when we were both studying in France. He was on the verge of returning home as a licensed veterinarian. I can still see him enlivening our Sunday student meetings. He was instrumental in helping me to overcome my feelings of inferiority, and led me to understand the necessity of independence, not just for my little country, but for all of Africa. Faced with my scepticism, he managed to convince me that this was more than just a Utopian vision. He drew

51

examples from world history and from contemporary Asia. Thanks to him I learned the relationship between politics and study: the impossibility of discussing politics without constant study and, inversely, that study is impossible without asking questions as to where the world is heading and, in the final analysis, without taking an active role in politics. I remember a phrase of his that I often repeated myself, as if I had been its author.

'If you don't *do* politics, you will be done in by it.'

At the time this apparently harmless statement had an immeasurably strong persuasive power over me, the adolescent whose mother had always said: 'Don't ever get involved in politics. It's a jungle of thieves and gangsters.'

When the *loi cadre** was passed and independence won, Ndoté clearly explained to me how it was all a farce, and how our president was no more than a stooge of French imperialism. The following year, when I no longer saw him at school and heard that he had returned home, I feared he would be arrested.

Six months later I read in the newspaper that he was appointed Ambassador to Tunisia. I never could understand how it happened. And now I found him Governor of this region.

We reminisced about the past and did not speak again of my reason for coming to see him.

'Tell me, what town are you from?' he asked me.   'Oh, that's a lovely town. I go there from time to time and like it very much. My wife talked about buying a house in that region.'

'Yes, it certainly is beautiful.' I said. 'But it's being neglected. The streets in the very centre of town are rutted and there have been no street lights for five years. The secondary school is inadequate ...'

---

*Law passed by the French government in 1956, which granted to the French overseas territory of the Middle Congo responsible government with an assembly elected by universal suffrage.

'Who is the mayor?'

'Zabouna.'

'Hum, … so. And who preceded him?'

'Old Ekodo.'

'Oh yes. He's dead now, isn't he?'

'Yes.'

'You know, it's all his fault that the township has deteriorated. He did absolutely nothing.'

I don't know exactly why, but I had the unpleasant suspicion that the Governor had only criticized the former mayor because he was no longer alive.

The telephone rang.

'Yes. Very good. Show him in.'

Mr Vuillaume entered. He wore a sporty nylon shirt hanging over his trousers, and sandals. I always find it ridiculous to see our government functionaries wearing dark, three-piece suits and ties to official ceremonies at times when these outfits make them sweat heavily in the hot sun. But I also find it unacceptable when a foreigner stands before one of our state officials dressed for the beach. I think if I had been in the Governor's shoes, I would have sent Mr Vuillaume home to get dressed.

'You see, Mr Vuillaume, I called you in to confirm something. Mr Dahounka here, whom you have already met I believe, is an envoy of our national government. He was assigned to inquire into certain aspects of the financial structure of IMA. It appears that you have refused him access to certain documents.'

'I believe I did my duty. I gave the inspector all the documents I have authority to give him. He wasn't satisfied, and requested others which are considered confidential and which I cannot possibly hand over without the express consent of our director.'

'But they are being requested by the Government, Mr Vuillaume.'

'Yes, so I understood. Then the State must contact our director who will subsequently give me the go-ahead.'

Ndoté nodded his head in an understanding way.

'Did you say to Mr Dahounka that you had no use for our Government?'

'No, I did not. I believe I said I was sorry not to be able to give satisfaction to the Government but that I was answerable directly to my superior.'

No longer able to restrain myself, I interrupted and remarked that his elegant manner of speech did not disguise his meaning. As a citizen I was hurt to see that an order from my Government made no impression at all on a foreigner. The conversation degenerated into a diatribe between Vuillaume and myself. His sarcastic tone bordered on insult. Several times I glanced at Ndoté and tried to catch his eye in support, but realized that he was ill-at-ease and would have preferred quietly to disappear behind his desk. Somehow he managed to regain control of the conversation.

'In the final analysis, it's not such a serious matter.'

I stood there, astonished.

'No, it's not serious. Just a misunderstanding, I think. Certainly Mr Vuillaume should have used more courteous language. But I cannot believe you really had unfriendly thoughts about our Government. As for you, dear friend, I understand perfectly well how you feel. If our Minister had not been in quite so much of a hurry and had let me know ahead of time, I could have provided you with a friendly introduction to IMA.'

Ndoté continued preaching thus for five minutes and then dismissed the matter. Finally he got up and accompanied Mr Vuillaume to the door of his office. I heard him say:

'I'll see you this evening.'

'This evening?' asked Mr Vuillaume, astonished.

'Yes. Aren't you invited over to Mrs de Creatrix' house? I'll be there too.'

And he placed his hand on Mr Vuillaume's shoulder as he opened the door.

'What else did you expect? We really can't do anything about it. True, his is an imperialist attitude, yet if we don't let the matter drop, they'll blow it up out of all proportion and tomorrow their country will take reprisals and cut our aid. Yes, my dear friend, it isn't easy. But should he start in again, then I won't miss my chance.'

The more I think about it, the less I feel like writing my report. Maybe someone will read it. Maybe they will even pound the table. Then they will quietly file away the documents. Vuillaume will not be sent out of the country. IMA will continue to run a lucrative business. I am up against an entire social structure that must be knocked down. One day it will happen. And when it does, I don't know what will become of a gentleman as charming and honourable as Ndoté.

THE ADVANCE

'No good,' the little girl said, screwing up her face.

'Yes it is, Francoise. Look.' Carmen herself swallowed a mandarin section, then closed her eyes. The little girl looked at her, impassively.

'Eat it all up.'

Like a priest proffering the host, Carmen offered her the orange quarter. Haughtily, the little girl turned her head away. It was already seven o'clock. Carmen was eager to finish up her work, especially since she had not yet asked the mistress ...

She spoke more sharply and looked stern.

'If you don't eat, Francoise, I'm going to tell your mother.' Still the little girl did not relent.

The mistress of the house was in the living room, together with her husband, entertaining friends they had invited over for bridge. She had already warned Carmen several times not to bother her when she was, as she said, 'with company'. Did Carmen dare to interrupt the happy group anyway? She did not fear being yelled at. People raise their voices mostly to relieve their own tensions. And since, according to Ferdinand the watchman, Madam's husband beat her, she took her revenge out on the servants. Why feel resentful? It was far better to just accept it philosophically. But to be taken to task in front of others, strangers, that was worse than being slapped. So Carmen preferred to wait.

Also, Madam had the annoying habit of speaking to her daughter as if she were an adult.

'Francoise, sweetheart, what did you have to eat?' And little Francoise, while reciting for her mother, would delight in explaining that she had not eaten any dessert because the mandarins Carmen wanted to give her were rotten. And Madam would admonish Carmen for not having told her about it. Especially since she had already explained that without dessert the child might not get a well-balanced meal, and so on and so forth. Carmen would usually listen to it all, seriously. In her village, and over in Makélékélé, what mattered was that a child had a full belly and did not go hungry. If, in addition, they had to worry about a balanced diet, there would never be an end to it. Besides, Carmen must not forget to ask her mistress …

There was only one solution. Do as her own mother had done to get her to eat. With one hand she opened the child's mouth and with the other shoved in the piece of fruit. As expected, Francoise howled. She cried and choked with rage. From the hallway came hammer-like sounds on the tile floor – the footsteps of Madam who came running. Carmen had won.

'What's going on in here?'

'She doesn't want to eat, Madam.'

'Oh don't force her, poor little thing. Get her some grapes from the refrigerator. She likes grapes.'

Madam took the little girl's head in her hands and kissed her several times. Carmen went to get the European-style dessert. As she was returning, she crossed Madam in the hall and almost broached the subject that was on her mind. But it did not seem like quite the right moment.

Francoise ate the grapes with relish. They must be good because instead of being her usual, talkative self, she remained calm and quiet as she ate the fruit. One day Carmen would have to swipe some of them and see what they tasted like.

While the little girl ate, Carmen wiped the tears from her cheeks. In her heart she cared a great deal for this child. Carmen had been with her since she was two months old and had practically brought her up. Francoise was as much her daughter as Madam's. Even if she quit her job, or Madam fired her, she would not be able to resist returning from time to time to see how Francoise had grown.

Then Carmen took the little girl to spend a penny, changed her, and put her to bed. By then it was 7.30. Night had fallen and she would still have an hour's walk to reach Makélékélé. But Francoise did not want her maid to leave. She clung to her annoying routine of wanting Carmen to sing her to sleep with a song.

> *'Nguè kélé mwana ya mboté,*
> Sleep baby sleep,
> Sleep baby sleep.'

After that she had to sing another. Usually the child would fall asleep during the second song but that evening it took three. While Carmen sang, her thoughts were elsewhere. She thought about Francoise whom she loved as much as her son, a child of the same age yet so different. Francoise was the picture of health, while her son had come close to death several times already. Nothing intimidated Francoise, she was comfortable speaking with grown-ups, ordered about the servants and already showed a certain fussiness in her choice of clothes. Her Hector did not dare to speak. He was shy and withdrawn with strangers. His unhappiness already showed in his eyes. Yet both children were of the same generation. They spoke the same language but would they be able to understand each other? Carmen did not think this jealously. No, she would like Hector to be 'well brought up', but how could that possibly be? Society and human nature would have to change.

That morning she had been very tempted to stay home from work. All night long the poor little fellow had cried. He complained of a stomach ache. He had diarrhoea and vomited at least three times. The first time seemed to relieve him, but the last brought something greenish up from his little stomach. Then his stomach continued to contract spasmodically and nothing more came up. The child was clearly in pain. His breathing was laboured, his forehead covered with sweat. She was very frightened and thought of the two children she had already lost. She even panicked. She had almost awakened her mother, asleep in the same compound. But she restrained herself. Her mother would have taken him immediately to the fetishist. That was how it happened with the other two. And they died. Yet each time she paid the equivalent of her own earnings. And after their deaths it was worse. The fetishist concluded she kept losing her children because for five years she had been refusing to marry the man her parents had chosen for her. And, in addition to her grief, she was obliged to suffer the nonsense of a relentless succession of old hags who harped on the subject, and tried to pressure her into yielding and giving in to either the will of God, the ancestors, the spirits, or her poor children. She should marry Kitonga Flavien and then everything would be all right again. Wasn't he a good catch? Besides his job as a government chauffeur, he was his own boss after work. He owned four taxis, a shop and a bar in Ouenze-Indochina. Kitonga would support her, she wouldn't have to work any longer. Besides, he already had two wives. One at Bacongo and the other who ran the bar at Ouenze.

While she contemplated all this, her son called. He wanted to sleep on her mat. He was afraid to be alone. Would he last until morning? When some children are sick their parents can immediately pick up the phone, dial a number and go straight to the doctor who does whatever is needed, or reassures them. But not poor people! The closest dispensaries are closed at night. And at the hospital we are received by a nurse who is rude and makes a fuss because we dared to wake him. As for going to a doctor, well, folks who live in the better parts of town won't open their doors at night to just anyone. Besides, she is letting her imagination run wild. A visit to a private doctor costs money.

Finally, at dawn, the child fell asleep. As for Carmen, she had to get up and go to work. Everyday she must walk two

59

hours from Makélékélé to Mipla. Since her mistress wants her to be there before 7.30, it's easy to calculate …

Despite her exhaustion she did not want to stay in bed. But neither did she want to go to work that morning. She would have preferred to go to the hospital and find out exactly what was wrong with Hector. Whenever he was ill, Carmen did not like to leave him alone. Her heart was not at ease. Once she tried to take him along to work, but Madam had made it plain that she was not being paid to care for her own son but for Francoise. Carmen knew that her mother and the other female relatives would take him to see a doctor. The tribal family is large and a child, no matter what happens, is never alone. But nonetheless, she believed that a child is best off being brought up by its mother. And those we have brought into the world need us most of all when they are sick.

But if she had devoted the day to her son, she would have been fired and then how would they manage? She had already missed work twice that month. The first time she really had been sick and had spent two feverish days on her mat. The second time was for a funeral. Madam was very angry.

'Carmen, I have had just about enough! Each time I need you, you aren't here. It almost seems as if you do it on purpose. You choose to stay home the very days I've made plans. My dear woman, I'm warning you now. If you miss one more day this month, you'll have to look for work elsewhere.'

How could she explain? Carmen tried her best. But white people, they think that whenever we don't come to work, it's because we're lazy.

And today she came to work despite Hector being so ill. At noon her sister sent word that the doctor had prescribed some medicine. It was always the same old story. How would she pay for it? Yet Hector must be cured.

And that evening, there she was, singing for a little girl who had everything, and whose parents were playing cards with other ladies and gentlemen.

When Francoise had fallen asleep, Carmen went to wait in the kitchen until the guests had finished their game of bridge.

60

She spent the time talking to Ferdinand, the old watchman. Those were moments she generally enjoyed. It lightened her spirits, eased her worry. They exchanged gossip on the shortcomings of their employers. Usually when Ferdinand described things he had seen, he would mimic them and Carmen would laugh. That evening, however, she remained serious and Ferdinand remarked on it.

Finally Madam came into the kitchen.

'Haven't you left yet Carmen?'

It was the most difficult moment. 'Madam, I need some money.'

'Again? But I paid you only ten days ago.'

'My son is sick. He needs medicine.'

'Listen to that, just listen to that! So I am now the public welfare fund. They have children without a husband and then they can't manage to take care of them!'

'Madam, white people say that ...'

'So your child is sick? Well, it's because you don't listen to me. I've told you again and again that you must feed him properly. Did you do it?'

'No, Madam.'

'No, of course not. It's easier to fill his stomach with your rotten old *manioc*.'

What could Carmen answer? That she had tried the diet Madam suggested but it was beyond her means. It seemed that Madam did not realize how in one week she spent three times Carmen's monthly salary just to feed her husband, her daughter, herself and their cat. If the maid had reminded her of that, she would have been fired for insolence.

'But anyway, I don't have any cash at home this evening. When will you natives understand that money doesn't grow on trees? When will you learn to put money aside and save?'

And Madam continued speaking like that for a long time. Carmen did not understand all she said. When people speak French too rapidly, she doesn't have time to translate it all in her mind, so she just tunes out and nods her head, as she did at that moment. Had that perhaps softened Madam? In any

61

case, she gave her some aspirin and promised her 500 francs the following day.

So finally black Carmen left. She walked all the way back to Makélékélé. It was far from Mipla to Makélékélé. As far as from her native village to where she was sent to school. It left plenty of time for thought.

Carmen wanted to run, she felt so strongly that Hector needed her. But after not having slept the whole night, and eating nothing but a slice of *manioc* for lunch, she could not run. Suddenly she felt that Hector was calling her.

Poor little thing. 'When he grows up, will he love me? To support us both I must leave him alone all day long. Maybe he'll resent it. I regret having left him without medical care so long. But I had faith in the white man's medicine and in his good will. If Mamma suggests I take him to the fetishist tonight, I won't be able to refuse any longer.'

And she thought about all Madam had said. They would never really understand each other. Carmen spent more time with her mistress than with her own son. Madam entrusted her daughter to Carmen in complete confidence. And yet Carmen could not understand Madam's reactions nor could Madam imagine what was going on in her maid's head, or the difficulties of her world. She considered Carmen an irresponsible and frivolous girl.

How does she expect me to save money on 5000 francs a month. Last month she only paid me 4000. For six months now she has been keeping back 500 francs a month to help repay the cost of the watch I bought. It was my only extravagance. Then I had to give 1000 francs to the *tontine** of our community, 1000 francs to my mother, 1000 francs to pay for the trip home of my aunt and cousins who had moved in with us for a month. I had only 1000 francs left. And what is 1000 francs? Madam spends that much on food every day.

*Community-based method of saving. Every month, each participant contributes a fixed sum. The entire amount is handed over monthly, in turns, to one of the members.

Cars passed by in the poorly lit streets. Those that came towards Carmen blinded her with their headlights. Those that arrived from behind barely missed hitting her. And no one stopped to give her a lift. Yet she knew that at least half of the cars were driven by blacks like herself. In today's world, each to his own.

Oh, if only Madam would remember to give her money for the medicine tomorrow.

As she approached Biza Street, the cry of women's voices raised in the night reached her:

> *'Mwana mounou mê kouenda hé!*
> *Hector hé,*
> *Mwana mounou mê kouenda hé.'*

She understood that medicine or fetishist, it was too late.

> 'Oh my son has gone away!
> Oh my Hector,
> Oh my son has gone away.'

WHISKEY

On the fifteenth floor of the hotel, along the bank of the chocolate coloured river, Kalala let the cool wind penetrate his body, caress his face. He even felt slightly chilled. Impassive in his chair, he drew deeply on a cigarette. He was on the terrace – unless he was on the water or elsewhere.

The fifteenth floor houses the bar, where every evening a local band plays to the white technical attachés and peace corps volunteers. For that reason the musicians do not play the typical hip-shaking local music. No high life, no Congolese tunes, no *beguine*. The band plays for the white patrons – the blues, the jerk, rumbas, waltzes. Once or twice during the evening, mostly for relaxation, the musicians take on a *pachanga*. The rhythm shakes them awake, and the awkward way the white people dance to the Afro-Cuban tune amuses them. At the moment, however, the band members were playing music which did not move them. They were not making love to their instruments. One could feel it. They were selling their music for the pleasure of the twentieth century civilian equivalent of the Byzantine Empire centurions. They are prostituting themselves, thought Kalala.

The band had just finished a waltz. In the silence that followed, Kalala heard a continuous crackling noise. Was it the hotel's battery of air conditioners or the rushing of the river's rapids alongside the hotel?

Kalala was seeking peace and quiet. He found it nowhere. All around were diversions which only irritated him. Whenever he thought he found silence, there was always something

64

which shocked him, awakened his thoughts, revolted him. He had not come to the fifteenth floor that evening because he found the night-club atmosphere relaxing. No, he had come to get whiskey, the hateful drink so typical an element of the colonial rule. He needed to drink that evening, after all that he had gone through. That evening prior to his rendezvous.

At six a.m. when he had awakened to take his morning constitutional in the hospital courtyard before making the rounds of his patients, someone awaited him on the veranda. It was cousin Pina, the drunkard, whom Kalala alternately considered a cousin and a stray. Now he would miss his exercise. Kalala almost shouted at him that it was not the proper time for a visit. But something serious might have happened. He had better listen first.

They embraced.

'What is it Pina?'

'Here, I brought you a duck and some yams, your favourites.'

Obliged to swallow his anger, Kalala smiled and thanked his cousin. Once again Pina had won. Would Kalala never find the occasion to tell him how drink was destroying him?

Pina, feeling at ease, introduced the man who accompanied him.

'We were friends at school. For eleven years he has been teaching in the bush without complaint. Today his inspector transferred him to another position. With eleven children imagine what that means ...'

School had already begun three weeks earlier. Kalala nodded.

'Who is covering your class today?'

'No one.'

Kalala nodded again. The teacher did not feel conscience-stricken. He was only demanding his due.

'And what do you expect me to do?'

Pina was the one to answer.

'The Minister of Education's office manager was a fellow student of yours. You know each other. I even saw him here once. He is from our tribe. I imagine he could do something.'

65

Pina's friend continued.

'The truth, Doctor, is that I was named head of the teacher's union in our region. That angered the inspector. Since, at the same time, he wanted to place a young tribal brother in the town to spy for him, I became, Doctor, a damaged article to be exchanged for first quality goods. I was treated like a piece of human merchandise, subject to underhand manipulation. The place they want to send me is a hell on earth. Usually teachers are sent there to work off punishment.'

My goodness, can't the man speak more simply?

'Don't the children living in that hell have the right to an education?' burst out Kalala, unable to control himself any longer. Then abandoning his two visitors on the veranda, he went to prepare for his hospital rounds.

He crossed the courtyard which separated his home from the tall building ahead. This was one of his favourite times of day. The sun was not yet up. The cool air whipped against his face and made his blood rise. These few minutes of purification always brought to mind the athletic training grounds on a cool morning.

But as soon as he climbed the stairs, a mixture of odours accosted him: sweat, drugs, food, even excrement. In this place, where it should have been of major concern, the patients, nurses, as well as the hospital workers, seemed unaware of the importance of cleanliness. It had been that way since a 'fellow national' was named director of the hospital. His first task had been to transfer much of the personnel, replacing them with members of his family and people from his own village. To ensure that workers at all levels were devoted to him, he said. As was evident, this resulted in everyone doing things his own way.

Kalala visited each of his patients. Due to a shortage of beds some were doubled up two a bed. Wardrobes were even turned over to serve as beds, made up with sheets and blankets to accommodate other patients. As he passed each bed, Kalala wondered whether he were really being a doctor. He did nothing more than relieve pain. Once out of the hospital, most patients would return to situations favouring the recurrence of their ailments: poor or insufficient nourishment, unsanitary living conditions, not to mention those whose lives, indelibly marked by conditions of their childhood, were destined to be cut short. And then there was ignorance and superstition to deal with, which would negate all the benefits of scientific medicine. Once the medical treatment was completed, the patient would visit the fetishist and there ... the real doctor would be the whole army of patients. Did this army want to break out from its concentration camp? Was it ready to move along a path capable of shaking it up?

Kalala was reminded of his meeting a few weeks earlier with the electric company's director on his large, neon-lit veranda. They were old school colleagues and had shared *manioc* and salted fish together in the dormitories. Nzodi. He had studied in eastern Europe for seven years and received his degree in engineering. His training 'behind the iron curtain' resulted in his being black-listed on his return home. But Nzodi was from the same village as the President and therefore a brother. He was the first young professional to prove that in Africa, tribal connections are stronger than ideology, even ideological ties based on class struggle.

They sat on the veranda, Nzodi drinking his whiskey and soda, Kalala his ever-present orange juice. Kalala had been obliged to wait a good two hours for the departure of the other visitors (who did not speak at all and must have come to ask for money) before introducing the real issue he wanted to discuss.

'Hey, Nzodi, did you hear our esteemed leader's talk on Sunday?'

'Yes,' and he laughed.

'Didn't it alarm you?'

'Oh, you know, since my return, nothing surprises me. Those are just the f-a-c-t-s o-f l-i-f-e in this country. Perhaps the truth is that I think about it less than I used to. With this system of round the clock workday, I'm up at five in the morning. At one o'clock, when I leave the office, I have two cocktails which help me sleep until four. In the evening, before nightfall, I go across the tracks, get my fill of the crowds and see how my childhood girl friends have grown. I engage in discreet 'politicking' with the ones I find most attractive, and by seven I'm at home where I devote myself to my wife until morning. But I prefer to leave politics, as the term is understood here, alone.'

'Even so, you can't possibly remain indifferent to that talk.'

'I tell you, I just don't want to think about it anymore. Since my return home, I haven't even unpacked all those books by Engels, Mao and the others. The same goes for Shakespeare, Aragon, Cesaire – and – Tolstoy. I only read detective stories. I think if I read any of them, even Tolstoy or Ghandi, I would feel compelled to fashion Molotov cocktails and blow this whole damn society sky high. And what would I gain by it? I would be arrested, strung up by the neck in the city square, declared a martyr. But where in all that is the revolution? Our people aren't ready yet, my friend. Apart from my family, they would all come to cheer on the tyrant. In Africa, the winner is the one who gets the acclaim. It has nothing to do with being right. If today you were president and I were in prison, everyone would applaud you as "the father of our country". I would be labelled a "traitor". If tomorrow, you were to fall and I to be released from prison, the same crowds who cheered you would now bestow on me the title of national hero. As I said, only your family remains loyal. Not because it shares your ideas, but because of pure brute sentimentality. And after your death, if your executioner compensates your relatives richly enough, they will be satisfied. Look at Pauline Lumumba today ...'

Kalala succeeded in returning to the President's talk only with great difficulty.

'My dear fellow, the "boss" is a sly old fox. He understands the masses perfectly. Knows how to manipulate them better than any of us intellectuals.'

Kalala tried to show him the dangers that existed precisely because the 'captain' played up to certain habits, certain practices of the people.

'Traditions are static. They don't move things along. They don't help a crowd which nonetheless needs to change. All his attacks against the "educated elite" are just a pretence for denouncing the intellectuals in justification of his arbitrary arrest of Epayo.'

Epayo was a young lawyer, first of the original generation of university graduates to return to the country. Six years ago, the President arrested him for conspiring against the State. He was found guilty and condemned to death. For two years there was no word of him. Then his sentence was commuted to twenty years of hard labour. Last year, upon returning from a trip to the US where he received promises of aid, the President granted him amnesty.

And now, while pleading the case of a thief last week, Epayo declared to the court that the 'continuing economic and social degradation of our country was becoming daily more distressing. It is the reason behind the appearance in the cities of a lower class, to which my client belongs. These people live like nomads on the fringe of the city. They stand ready to clash with our more affluent citizens who live in the better parts of town. Today they are committing larceny ...'

The clerk of the court hailed from the same village as the President. He had entrance to the presidential palace both night and day, even when the door remained closed to some of the Cabinet Ministers. At that moment he was in financial straits, having to pay the hospital bills for his mistress who had just given birth. He reported the speech to the Chief of State who noted that, once again, Epayo had criticized the economic, social and political situation of the country. The clerk received his envelope and, the same night, Epayo was arrested at his home. Not until three days later – in his Sunday evening address – did the President officially announce Epayo's arrest and the discovery of a new conspiracy led by agents in the pay of a foreign totalitarian power.

Nzodi knew Epayo well. Before leaving to study in the socialist countries, he and Epayo had been political activists together in France, members of the radical left-wing FEANF.* At that time, Nzodi was president of the Toulouse branch. Epayo, although always present at the meetings, had categorically refused to assume any leadership position. He invariably answered:

'I'll leave all that to those who have greater stamina than I do. My first duty as an activist is to finish my studies as rapidly as possible and return home.'

Nzodi had been the one to label Epayo as suspect, not really devoted to the movement. Yes, he could not possibly have forgotten him. Often when he thought back to that time, Nzodi considered it one of the best in his life. The one, in any case, when he had given the best of himself to what he considered a noble cause. He could still remember hiding Algerian comrades who were being hunted, and going from door to door collecting signatures on a petition which demanded freedom for Djamila Bouhired, the first Algerian woman terrorist to have bombed a café for the freedom of her country. Every Sunday he sold the French Communist Party newspaper. He spent long hours trying to change the minds of his fellow students who refused to sign petitions from fear of losing their scholarships.

But whenever his memories became too haunting, Nzodi turned to drink.

Had he become a traitor to the movement? He alone knew. Whenever former colleagues asked him this question, he replied in the negative. It was merely a question of facing up to the reality of the country's situation. He was part of a sacrificed generation which would be worn out by heavy responsibilities. The following generation, the one to launch the revolution, would not be made up of people like himself.

Kalala's words came to him as if from an unreal dream which disturbed his sleep.

*Federation of Black African Students in France

'Let me repeat that I do not think we have the right to leave Epayo in this situation. However feeble the means at our disposal, we must somehow awaken public opinion, force people to think. We must offer an alternative to the favouritism which currently runs rampant.'

From his briefcase he removed a sheet of paper which he unrolled on the table. He handed Nzodi a pen.

'Go ahead. You must sign. It's a petition. Already three of us have signed it. If fifteen former students put their names at the bottom, "he" cannot arrest us. You have to do it, old man.'

Nzodi did not answer. He uncorked the bottle of whiskey and offered it to Kalala, who declined by covering his glass with his hand. Nzodi poured himself out a generous drink and downed a mouthful. Then he lit a cigarette and inhaled deeply. There was a long, uncomfortable silence.

'You know,' began Nzodi, 'in this sort of affair one never knows exactly what lies behind it. Maybe – I don't mean to say that Epayo actually conspired against the government – but maybe he had really prepared something. And did he consult us? How can we compromise our positions by supporting someone when, in the final analysis, we don't really know for whom or with whom he worked? I think the best way to proceed is to form a delegation of two or three people who will meet with the Chief of State and ask him for an explanation. But to try to employ here the methods we used in France … He shook his head – no.'

Finally Kalala stood up and left.

The following day, Kalala visited six other former students. They had all forgotten the words which formerly, in a more temperate climate, had been so familiar to their lips. Now each one exhibited a great wisdom. A very strange wisdom, in truth.

Finally Kalala returned to Nzodi and asked him to arrange a meeting with the President.

***

They sat in what had formerly been the waiting room of the

colonial government. Kalala and Nzodi were sweating in the suits they felt obliged to wear out of respect for the Chief of State. Facing them, in short sleeves, were a French colonel and another military man who had not even bothered to don their uniform jackets. The colonel frequently glanced at the two friends as if they had penetrated a sacred place to which they should have been denied access. From time to time a European passed by in the corridor and seeing the colonel, stopped to present his respects.

'Various technical advisers of the President', Nzodi explained. They seemed to be the only people in the building. He urged Kalala not to take offence. 'These people know our country well and love it. Although I am sorry to have to say so, they are more competent than our own citizens. Besides, since the President travels so extensively outside the country to keep a high international profile, the Government could not function without the continuity and stability assured by the advisers.'

Two Europeans, also in shirt sleeves, left the President's office. Their faces wore contented, idiotic smiles. From their looks one guessed they were former paratroopers who had arrived in Africa during the colonial era and stayed on after demobilization to earn their fortunes in some business or other. Kalala recognized in them that mentality which, in France, would have inhibited them from facing even a simple teacher without stammering. Here they were received at least once a month by the Chief of State without feeling the least compulsion to so much as wear a tie. They had no greater respect for their hosts, the country's inhabitants. Their attitude had not changed one iota since independence. Each of the two men carried in his hands a small model of a very elegant home.

'So,' questioned the colonel, 'which is it to be?'

'Both,' answered one of them, his face assuming an expression as if to say 'I just can't believe it.' He tried to appear naïve but could not hide his elation at the prospect of this unexpected profit. The colonel, with the dignity of his rank, merely nodded his head.

The same evening the entire French enclave would know that the President had ordered the construction of two personal residences.

The Chief of State's private secretary appeared (she too was French, young, beautiful and, according to rumour, full of admiration for her boss) and advised the colonel that the President was ready to see him.

Suddenly the Minister of Agriculture entered, speaking loudly and vehemently with a technical adviser who replied to him:

'I would be greatly surprised if the President could see you. He has a very busy schedule today.'

The Minister proceeded to enter the secretary's office. Ten minutes later he came back out, angry undoubtedly because he had not succeeded in arranging the sought-after meeting.

Two hours after the appointed time, Kalala and Nzodi were finally ushered in. The President indicated two seats which were placed in front of his desk. Nzodi spoke first. He presented the reasons for their visit in such a gentle, smiling way that Kalala could not resist interrupting him.

'Excuse me, Nzodi. Allow me please, Mr President. I would like to clarify the matter.' Although courteously phrased, his questions were so direct that the President was forced to respond.

'So you want proof?' He pressed a button. 'Bring me the file on Epayo,' he ordered his office manager.

As he waited for the file, the President spoke, becoming more and more agitated. He spoke of our traditions, of the totalitarian ideas introduced from outside which were completely foreign to our philosophy of life and to the traditional values of our black world.

'Epayo is a crook who wants to introduce communism here, accompanied by the Chinese who will come by the millions. No, my friends.' He stood up and beat his fist on the desk. 'I will not allow it. As long as I am in charge and the people are fortunate enough to have me as a leader, I will preserve our civilization from the corrupt influences of the white and yellow worlds.' His tirade wandered from village palavers and hospitality, to the pre-eminence of existence over possession. 'How do you imagine that with scientific socialism we could maintain the natural *joie de vivre* of the black world? They want to destroy our sense of community, our respect for the elders, our magical style and symbolism which echoes the cosmos, the strength of our faith, and finally our visual values and our orality. This young man is a piece of rotten fruit. If you leave one wormy orange in a basket of good ones, all become rapidly infested. No matter how beautiful the orange is, it must immediately be thrown out.'

The assistant returned with a folder that was, incidentally, very flat. He handed it to the President, who with a shout of victory, opened it and spread out the 'file' on Epayo.

Kalala saw there an anonymous letter, apparently sent from Paris, which cited the names of the principal dangerous communists. Epayo's name figured on the list. There was a police report claiming that Epayo had been seen at the airport greeting a high Guinean official who passed through. Another report questioned what went on in his office where people who posed as his clients came and went all day long. They were suspected of really being his agents stationed in other regions of the country. A police informer had once pretended to be a client and managed to enter the office but Epayo, being intelligent, had revealed nothing. Finally there was a photocopy of a letter Epayo was said to have sent to a relative who was then studying in France. Underlined were the following sentences:

'Everything continues as usual here. The "helmsman" leads us as best he can, more like the paddler of a dugout than the captain of a modern ocean liner. But the corrupt crew is submissive to him and the passengers dare not object. We are only waiting for the vessel to run aground before presenting an alternative ...'

'And that's not all,' roared the Chief of State. 'At a dinner with foreigners Epayo stated that a mere primary school teacher could never manage to govern a country. And the other day at the courthouse, he proclaimed that the political and economic situation was rotten and in consequence, revolution was the only answer.'

Then the President played them a tape which was purported to have been the confession of Epayo. In truth, Kalala was not able to recongize his friend's voice. Anyway, could a tape be taken as proof?

It was a discouraged and disgusted Kalala who left the building.

'See,' concluded Nzodi, 'we should have made sure of our information first.'

Kalala coldly bid him goodbye. He returned to the hospital, did not eat but went immediately to his office.

***

Kalala checked his watch. It would soon be midnight. The crowd in the night club had grown. At a table he saw four young women dressed in slacks, sporting wigs and smoking. They would probably enjoy dancing the be-bop that the orchestra was playing at the moment, he thought. He approached the most slender, who wore a wig cut in a boyish style, and invited her to dance. He enjoyed dancing to the Charlie Parker tune, which reminded him of the intimate night-club atmosphere when jazz was king. Physically moving to the music induced in him the relaxation he greatly needed. Kalala let himself go. He executed all the steps he knew. The girl was visibly pleased and in her dignified way, carrying her head high, showed off what she could do. Although he was exhausted, Kalala danced the next number too. It was important that as many people as possible see him and, if necessary, be able to testify that he had spent the evening dancing at The Riverside.

When the music stopped, he left money in the saucer under the bill. Taking advantage of the dimmed lights and the large crowd on the floor for the slow number, he left. Outside, parked 300 feet from the hotel, was a black Peugeot 404 with its parking lights on. It was the car Kalala was awaiting. He lit a cigarette, and with measured steps walked towards the car. When he drew alongside the 404, a door opened. He slipped in and they moved off.

In the back, Kalala recognized two colleagues with whom he had worked during the previous few days. One of them handed him his package of leaflets.

When they arrived at the African section, the whole town was asleep. They left the main street and took quieter, unpaved side roads. The three who were not driving began throwing leaflets out of the window, leaflets they had written, typed and duplicated themselves. Two other groups were covering other sections of the city. What a surprise the next morning when the inhabitants would find the tracts on their doorsteps! How it would anger the President!

After driving around for fifteen minutes, and with only one street left to do, the driver noticed that a car was following them. They stopped throwing out the tracts. The driver slowed down to allow the car behind to pass. It slowed down too. He sped up. It did the same. Probably the police, and the chase was on.

The pursuers were having great difficulty keeping up, when suddenly the driver yelled out.

'Damn!'

He had just noticed he was on a dead end street. A sign 300 feet ahead, 'Road Closed Men at Work' forced him to brake sharply. The only thing left to do was climb out of the car.

'Hands up!'

Bright lights were shined in their faces. A French police officer, accompanied by three African policemen, surrounded them, automatic rifles in hand.

The policemen cursed Kalala and his friends, and cursed their mothers, then forced them into the patrol wagon which had been tailing them. Kalala actually landed flat on his stomach. One of the policemen had shoved him the back with his night stick. The pain burned.

Kalala looked down at his hands. They were handcuffed. Yet inside he felt light, free, just the way he had felt as a child leaving confession. That feeling was the most important thing – better than the whiskey, better than the pop music of the early evening.

THE CONSPIRACY

How can I convince my colleagues to stop …?

Yet I myself was so sure. For two years I have written reports on him but the Director never lent any weight to them. In summing up the facts of the case, he excluded everything concerning Dr Mobata. In his opinion there was never enough concrete evidence.

I don't know what accounted for his attitude since, after all, he and Mobata were not tribal brothers.

But finally I had in hand solid information which would enable me to put this agent from Moscow behind bars and prove that the communists, together with a foreign power, were behind the whole business. And coming just a few months prior to the presidential elections, it would undoubtedly be worth a promotion.

I tingled with anticipation. I gathered together copies of all my reports to brandish in my boss' face. I had constantly reminded him that Mobata was a communist, that he organized a network, and that very often, under the guise of a medical consultation, he held secret meetings in his office.

Even the Director himself didn't deny that Mobata was 'red', an ardent communist. Hadn't he studied in Russia? It was in his file. And despite this, the Director shielded him, saying he was a trained professional, much needed and in short supply in our country. A man's ideas can't be changed. To believe in communism isn't illegal, as long as one doesn't organize a clandestine movement to overthrow the government in power. According to him, the doctor was an idealist who would come around to more reasonable political ideas in time and with greater experience. In any case, the best way to encourage this conversion was to not prosecute him.

And then this business came to light. A group of conspirators planned to arouse the populace and overthrow the regime. Nabangou, the leader, managed to escape, but we captured most of the commandos who were to have carried out the coup.

I first smelled something fishy when one of our men pointed out to me that a notebook belonging to a conspirator contained Dr Mobata's name. Evidently, taken alone, this wasn't proof. But then Mobata's house boy decided to talk. He claimed that Nabangou, the leader of the conspiracy, came for an appointment every day during the week preceding the attempted coup, and each time the doctor spent almost an hour with him, attention not usually accorded to other patients.

Finally, there was not a shadow of a doubt. I could hardly sit still and itched to make sure the bird did not fly the coop. I decided to take charge myself of the delegation sent to arrest him. If it had been up to me, I would have moved immediately. But, once again, the Director delayed the operation with intellectual arguments that had been drilled into him during his study and training in Europe. 'A man should not be arrested in his home at night.' So we had to wait until morning. The night seemed endless.

Mobata did not protest, as if he knew our nerves were on edge and we were only waiting for the slightest provocation to crack him across the face. He took his time, probably to demonstrate he was not afraid.

He kissed his wife who clung to him for a moment and said something to her I could not make out. I think it was in their native tongue, which I do not understand. Then he bent down to hug his child and looked at him for a long moment.

'Get a move on. We have no time to waste,' I cried.

I couldn't stand this show of affection. Those intellectuals are all the same. They have such emasculating habits. Or maybe they are trying to soften us up, prove to us that with the noble sentiments they display towards their family and others, their cause can't help but be just and humane. On the staircase I shoved him about a little. He almost fell.

'Be careful. I'm not an animal.'

'Move on and shut your trap.'

I didn't want to be preached at. If nothing else, it was the wrong moment and I wouldn't have stood for it. He had just gotten up and would have stayed in bed another hour that Sunday morning if we hadn't been so rude as to drag him from it. While I, for two nights, had been unable to sleep.

When we arrived at my office, I put my pistol on the table and glared at him. He didn't react. My nerves were electrified.

'Sit down, Doctor. Don't worry. We don't want to harm you. At least not if you co-operate. I assume you know why we've brought you here?'

'I have no idea. But I suppose you will tell me.'

'Listen here, Doctor. We police are human beings. We understand the people we arrest. But we don't like to waste our time. If you talk, we'll lay off, and take it into account.'

'If you speak more plainly, I'll understand you better.'

'Cut the bravery!' I think I struck my fist on the table. 'Cut the bravery or we'll soon see who is stronger.'

Inspector Nzengo interrupted.

'Come on, own up. What part did you play in the conspiracy? Who were the other leaders? If you give me the right answer, we'll leave you in peace.'

'What conspiracy?'

'Oh, so you want to play dumb?' My foot pressed a button under the desk and a white floodlight blinded the doctor.

'How many conspiracies are there?'

'...'

'What do you take me for, an idiot? Don't you know that a group led by Nabangou almost succeeded in wiping us all out the other night?'

'I heard about it on the radio.'

'Oh, is that so? Tell me more. So you heard about it on the radio!'

'Just barely, too, I might add. You know, I have so much work that I don't devote as much time to politics as I would like.'

'How do you explain then, that your name and address were found in the notebook of one of the men picked up? And that recently, Nabangou came to your office every day for a week?'

This time the doctor was visibly shaken.

'Ah-hah … So you see, you'd better talk. We know all about you, my friend. You might as well own up while you still have the chance.'

'But anyone can write a doctor's address in his notebook. What I do deny is having received Mr Nabangou in my office. I haven't treated him for at least a year.'

'What patients did you see last Wednesday?'

'…'

'Shall we refresh your memory?'

'Tell me, Inspector, what is the third word of the fifth line of our national anthem?'

'What do you mean by that remark?'

'But don't you know it?' insisted the doctor.

'…'

'Yet you've heard the anthem many times. It's the same when you ask me point-black the names of my patients. But if I could consult my appointment book …'

A slap in the face shut him up.

'Who the hell do you think you're kidding? Do you also deny being a communist? And that as a communist you're an enemy of the President? One evening during a dinner you said that he "sold out", those are your own words, he "sold out" to what you called "American capitalists".'

'I admit that …'

'Catch that. He admits. Get that, he admits to being a communist and an organizer of the conspiracy.'

'No. I admit that possibly during a conversation I said it seemed to me foreign capital …'

81

'Don't be a smart alec.'

He was really beginning to get on my nerves. I had not slept for two nights. I was running only on the hot coffee my wife sent from home in a thermos, and on an increased daily consumption of cigarettes. The slightest contradiction irritated me greatly. I had to discharge on someone the electric energy that was coursing up and down my spine.

I jumped on him, grabbed him by the collar and slapped him several times about the face, knocking off his glasses. I really shook him up. I thought he would give in. Yet he made a conscious effort to dominate his pain. I recognized his type. Outwardly weak, yet gifted with an iron will and stubborn as a mule. They prefer to die rather than give in.

'You said, Inspector, ... you said just now I was a communist.'

'It is not *I* that said it. It's the truth.'

'I don't exactly deny it ...'

'Hear that. Get it down, please.'

'How could I collaborate with Nabangou who is an advocate of tribalism?'

'Cut the crap! Who the hell do you think I am to believe that crap!' I yelled at the top of my voice. 'We are the ones asking the questions here, not you.'

The telephone rang. The Director wanted to see me.

'OK, fellows. I'll be right back. Take care of him. I'm sure it will jog his memory a little.'

I left him in the hands of Zakunda and Mibolo, two interrogation experts. One of them had worked with the French in Algeria, where he had learned a whole battery of techniques. The other, I had to admit, was basically a sadist. Every month he dreamed up more and more refined means of torture.

When I entered, the Director pushed away the book he had been reading. He never read law books or detective stories, but always serious books which looked boring as hell. I could make out the title. *Comrade General Sun* by J. Stephen Alexis*.

Compère Général Soleil, a novel based on leftist revolutionary activity in the Caribbean.

He motioned me to a chair.

'Inspector, I see you have arrested Dr Mobata.' He lit a cigarette and inhaled deeply. 'Is he involved in this conspiracy too?'

'We found his address on one of the prisoners. You will admit that it's suspicious.'

The Director seemed unconvinced. But I could tell he was ill-at-ease. He dared not look me in the face. Although he had begun by plunging right into the middle of the case, he continued by beating around the bush. He spoke about his dislike of torture. Said it pitted the accused against his accusers, so that from being lukewarm opponents when brought in, they became vicious once released.

He considered torture degrading. He was charged with overseeing the security of the State, not with reducing men to the level of animals.

'But he's not a man. He's a communist.'

The Director did not answer but gave me a look more devastating than if he had cursed me.

'Sir, you don't make our job any easier. And you know it's difficult to explain to our men. If they had their own way, they would purely and simply do away with all the prisoners.'

'It's our duty to prevent them. We're the ones in charge, Inspector, not the frenzied mobs.'

And he launched into another of his long, moralistic speeches which I only half remember. Deep inside I thought: 'All this is nothing but intellectual argument. What more can be expected if we put doctors of law in charge of our internal security forces. Those guys have read too many books and their hearts are not really in the work. They think we can make the pig-headed bastards talk without making them hurt first.'

'And do you think if their *coup d'état* had succeeded, they would have let us go? Our heads would have been the first to fall, you can be sure of that. Turning the other cheek only works at Sunday School.'

The Director did not lack arguments to refute me. He spoke of the educational role of the police, the sadistic attitudes to be rooted out and replaced, and many other things which seemed removed from reality. I asked myself if he himself were not slightly pink around the edges.

In sum, he kept me in his office for two hours.

By the time he gave me leave to go, Zakunda and Mibolo had stopped working over the doctor. I found him stretched out on the floor, unconscious, with swollen eyes. A thin stream of blood flowed from his mouth. The guys reported he still hadn't talked.

It took three buckets of water to revive him. When he opened his eyes, he was like someone waking from a nightmare. He glanced at me with the look of a dying animal and blood flowed from his mouth.

'Will you talk now?' yelled Mibolo.

I stepped in. Even if the boss was wrong, I was obliged to carry out his orders. It was a concession I could make. The doctor was such a tough nut, it would be difficult to prove his ties with the conspirators. But it would be equally difficult for him to prove his innocence.

'Take him to his cell. Let him rot there till morning. Maybe he'll come to his senses overnight.'

I slept the whole night through. I needed to recuperate. The following morning I even arrived at work slightly late. The first things I asked for were the reports from the previous night's interrogations.

The man who carried the doctor's address continued to deny he knew Dr Mobata. In addition, the leader of the conspirators had been picked up. A patrol stopped him in a car sixty miles away. Disguised as a woman, he was recognized not far from the border. When caught, he confessed everything. Although repeatedly asked about the role played by Dr Mobata, he proclaimed the man's innocence.

But that doctor had the look of a conspirator!

There was a knock on the door. A police officer stood at attention, chest thrown out, head back. He saluted.

'At ease.'

'The Director asks to see you, Inspector.'

I found him relaxed. He spoke slowly and calmly about the conclusions drawn from the investigations. To support each statement, he showed me a document. It was obvious that Dr Mobata was not involved in the conspiracy. His house boy, who originally provided the information, had stammered when faced with Nabangou and then admitted that he made up the story partly in the hopes of getting some money and mostly to get even with his employer who had just fired him.

'My dear Inspector, I am giving you the honour of announcing his release to the doctor.'

The boss had won again. I fumed with rage. The police officer I sent to get Mobata sensed it. My discomfort only grew in the interval it took him to return. I decided to go myself to the cell on the lower floor.

As soon as I arrived, I knew something was wrong. The two policemen were bent down near the opened, heavy iron door of the cell. When they saw me, they stood up.

'What's happened?'

They didn't answer but pointed to the body stretched out on the floor. Dr Mobata had committed suicide. The classic coup of those incapable of facing torture. He had slit open a vein.

I think it was the first time a death had so affected me. I felt I was suffocating. My head was splitting apart. I wanted to yell out like a madman, beat the walls, and cry.

'What the hell do you think you're doing just standing there, you oafs. Get him out of here, quick!'

I shoved the policemen who had no idea what was going on. Of course the Director tore me off a strip. Nonetheless the State covered it up. An official version describing the cause of death was released. No one knows the truth.

But since that morning I have changed. For two days I couldn't eat. My wife said I was acting strangely. At first I just shrugged it off, but I saw too that the kids were looking at me in a funny way. When I hug them, I feel their innocent eyes searching mine to discover the secret hidden inside my head.

Maybe they too think I'm strange. I have asked to be transferred to a position in the bush. I no longer dare question suspects. It reminds me too much of the doctor and depresses me. But what makes me suffer most is that I don't know how to stop my colleagues from torturing. If I try, they just laugh in my face …

The African and Caribbean Writers Series

**The book you have been reading is part of
Heinemann's long established series of African and
Caribbean fiction. Details of some of the other titles
available are given below, but for further
information write to:
Heinemann Educational Books, 22 Bedford Square,
London WC1B 3HH.**

STEVE BIKO
I Write What I Like

'An impressive tribute to the depth and range of his
thought, covering such diverse issues as the basic
philosophy of black consciousness, Bantustans, African
culture, the institutional church, and Western involvement
in apartheid.'

The Catholic Herald

T. OBINKARAM ECHEWA
The Crippled Dancer

A novel of feud and intrigue set in Nigeria, by the winner
of the English Speaking Union Literature Prize.

BESSIE HEAD
When Rain Clouds Gather

In a poverty-stricken village in Botswana, the pressures of tradition, the opposition of the local chief and the harsh climate threaten to bring tragedy to the community.

ALEX LA GUMA
A Walk in the Night

Seven stories of decay, violence and poverty from the streets of Cape Town, and by one of South Africa's most impressive writers.

Time of the Butcherbird

In the intensifying summer heat, different members of a rural mining town community move inexorably towards conflict and ultimate tragedy. The time of the butcherbird is approaching.

'A most readable and moving book.'

West Africa

NELSON MANDELA
No Easy Walk to Freedom

A collection of the articles, speeches, letters and trials of the most important figure in the South African liberation struggle.

JOHN NAGENDA
The Seasons of Thomas Tebo

A pacy, vivid allegory of modern Uganda where an idyllic past stands in stark contrast to the tragic present.

NGŨGĨ WA THIONG'O
A Grain of Wheat

'With Mr Ngũgĩ, history is living tissue. He writes with poise from deep reserves, and the book adds cubits to his already considerable stature.'

The Guardian

NGŨGĨ WA THIONG'O
Devil on the Cross

Written while the auther was detained, without trial, by a government hoping to silence him. One of the most powerful critiques of modern Kenya ever written.

Petals of Blood

A compelling, passionate novel about the tragedy of corrupting power, set in post-independence Kenya.

'. . . Ngũgĩ writes with passion about every form, shape and colour which power can take.'

Sunday Times

SEMBENE OUSMANE
Black Docker

The leading Senegalese author and film maker draws on his own experiences and the problems of racism, prejudice and injustice to recreate vividly the uneasy atmosphere of France in the 1950s.

SEMBENE OUSMANE
God's Bits of Wood

The story of a strike on the Niger–Dakar railway, by the man who wrote and filmed *Xala*.

'Falling in the middle of Ousmane's literary canon, before he turned to film making, it is in some ways his most outstanding, and certainly his most ambitious work of fiction.'

West Africa

RICHARD RIVE
Buckingham Palace District Six

'Buckingham Palace' is dingy row of five cottages in Cape Town's notorious District Six. The neighbourhood is enlivened by a bizarre and colourful cast of characters, including Mary, the brothel keeper, Katzen, the Jewish landlord and Zoot, the charismatic 'jive king' of the area.

OLIVER TAMBO
Preparing for Power – Oliver Tambo Speaks

This selection of speeches, interviews and letters offers a unique insight into the ANC President's views on the history of the freedom struggle within South Africa, and of even greater importance his vision for the future.